The HOUSE *on* REDHILL CORNER

Dragonfly Publishing

BARBARA GURNEY

Copyright

Published by Dragonfly Publishing, October 2022

© All rights reserved by the author.

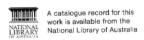
A catalogue record for this work is available from the National Library of Australia

Printed by: Pegasus Media & Logistics

ISBN (sc): 978-0-6454840-1-4
ISBN (e): 978-0-6454840-2-1

*"To shine your brightest light
is to be who you truly are."*

—Roy T. Bennett

One

Candice didn't wait for me to greet her but rushed through the open doorway, past me and into the lounge room. I followed, mumbling inadequate questions, hoping to find the reason for her red eyes and apparent despair.

Gasping for breath between sobs; twisting a tissue into a sodden ball, she sank onto the lounge. 'He never loved me.' She slowly shook her head, her eyes staring at nothing. 'Just walked out. Left. Jack's gone. Just like that.' She looked up. 'Asha, what'll I do?'

I responded automatically, 'Don't worry, we'll cleanse your spirit, and you can start afresh.'

Before I realised what I was doing, I stepped towards the cupboard that held the incense sticks, candles and crystals.

As I pulled a half-used candle from the drawer, I gulped in air. The candle fell to the floor. I stood still. Fireworks went off in my brain as my hands clasped my face.

I ignored my friend and shouted my way through my mother's home to my bedroom. 'No. I won't. I'm not Lalita. I'm not. Damn!'

Candy ran after me. 'Wait. I'm sorry. Please... wait.'

Pulling underclothes from drawers and tossing them on my bed, my anger eased. 'I'm sorry, Candy, but I've got to leave.'

She gripped my arm and shook it gently. 'It's alright, Asha. I shouldn't have said anything. Forget about Jack. I'm sorry.'

My body trembled. I stared at the socks scrunched up in my hand. 'No, I should be the one that's sorry.' I offered her one orange sock. 'You know I don't want to do that stuff. I don't want to be like Lalita. I just have to leave.'

With Candy's soothing repetition of comfort, I regained my equilibrium and calmed down. Jack's ears should have been burning as Candy recounted her misfortune to mistake that bastard's callous show of affection as the real thing. I hoped my murmurings of consolation helped, but my thoughts kept drifting. If I couldn't go anywhere right now, I would do some serious planning and some equally serious mind searching.

Two

Mr Cantronelli greeted me at the doorway of an old house on the corner of Redhill Road and Trowling Street. His mouth opened, and as if his teeth were about to be displaced, his bulbous lips sucked them back in quickly so he could form a smile.

'Good afternoon,' I said cheerfully, eager to get off on the right foot with my potential landlord.

'Yes, good afternoon, Miss.'

'I've come about the flat. The one with the sign in the window. Is it still vacant?'

'Of course. The little flat, it is vacant for some time. Come, you see.'

We trundled up the flight of stairs bounded by an enormous wooden balustrade. When we reached the first floor, he stood still for a moment to recover. 'Not like youngster anymore.' His gravelly voice broke into my thoughts, which had been soaking up the ambience.

'How old is this place?' I asked.

'Let me think of it.' He flapped his crinkly fingers in front of his face and took in a long breath before saying, 'I live up Trowling Street forty-five years ago. This house, it then a big family place. Had orchard in yard. The old orange tree by front door is only tree left. Twenty years they change it. I think it a shame. But there you go. Today everything be for money. They make old rooms into these flats, and here you go.'

After battling with numerous keys clipped to a long chain, he jiggled a brass key into the lock and stood back, waving in the direction of the empty room. As I entered, the large windows and ornate ceiling decorations charmed me.

'Wow! It's really nice.'

'This room be the old drawing-room. It is lovely, no?'

'Oh yes, it is definitely lovely. When can I move in?'

'You sure?' His intense gaze made me look away. 'You very sure?'

This repeated question bothered me. 'What's wrong with this place? Why wouldn't I want to move in?'

'No, no, nothing is wrong.' He fiddled with the keys and looked at the floor. I waited. 'People rent this place, and then they move out. I not know why. I just ask if you be sure.'

I glanced around the room again. The alterations to the old home were noticeable, giving an odd appearance to a once elegant room, but peculiar places don't bother me. I'd lived with meditating cushions sitting next to a television; dream-catchers holding shopping lists.

Mr Cantronelli shrugged. 'You like, you can have. Rent is very good price.'

I nodded and held out my hand. 'I'll take it. It's perfect.'

He ignored my hand but grinned and led me through to the bathroom. 'You check first, please.'

The inspection didn't take long. The large bedroom had a painted wardrobe in the corner. The carpet seemed recently cleaned. Evidence of a good scrubbing marked the small stove, and the narrow pantry would be adequate for my needs.

I didn't mind if other people had disregarded this little place; it had already welcomed me with its unmatched appearance and its attempt to fit in with the modern buildings next door.

I watched Mr Cantronelli lock the gravel-coloured door, excited by the prospect of owning the key he struggled with. The unique building had already wormed its way into my conscience.

The delicately carved handrail of the old staircase clashed with the pine doorframes. I'd noticed the architraves were incomplete, but the beige paintwork in the hallway looked fresh. The individually coloured doors of each flat made me smile.

Two days later, I moved in. Determined to add colour to the generic white-on-white, I bought several large posters for the walls. My new bed linen would help create a peaceful ambience of aqua and cream.

I travelled light, and it didn't take long before I had my meagre number of boxes scattered over a floor rug Candy's mum had donated.

Candy had forgiven me for my overreaction; we had grown up together. She understood.

The Hardwicks lived in the property adjoining our back fence. A central makeshift gate in a row of crooked pickets had survived despite Candy's father's promise of a better construction. Candy and I found it easy to live in one another's pockets. Even their dog used the two backyards.

I'd promised Bella and Candy they could help me unpack, so as I waited impatiently for their arrival, I located a few essential items and turned on the radio for company. Calming the mixture of excitement and nervous energy, I considered my mother's reaction to this change in our lives.

Three

My mother, with her newly chosen name of Lalita, was nineteen when I was born. While still in hospital, she blessed my arrival with the burning of myrrh incense and chanted a prayer to the universe as I lay squawking my lungs out. A nurse came running when she smelt something other than the hospital-strength disinfectant that usually permeated the rooms and tried to make Lalita Anglesea "stop all this nonsense and get back into bed".

'Goodness and light. Goodness and light,' Lalita continued to chant while the nurse doused the incense stick and pushed the new mother toward the neat white bed.

The other new mothers in the ward protested. One clutched a sheet to her nose and demanded Lalita be moved. Another buzzed for reinforcements.

For years, the atmosphere of contradiction continued as my mother instructed me on a life of spiritual enlightenment.

My father apparently felt his particular light needed to glow elsewhere and disappeared from the face of the universe. I never saw a photo or even heard tales of him. Any question I uttered to find the other half of my creation was met with systematic trivia. I quickly realised it was easier to stop asking questions.

I learnt to meditate by the time I was five–although I suspect I did a lot of daydreaming, as sitting cross-legged on a second-hand shagpile rug surrounded by a dozen lit candles would have become monotonous.

During my pre-teens, I tried to please the person who had been born Lorna Underwood by learning to tell the difference between a spell for cleansing the room and one promising to cleanse the soul of a believer.

It had been high excitement for the weeks leading up to my tenth birthday after my mother promised me my first party. I invited six girls from school, along with Candy and Bella, and to my delight, they all replied in the positive.

I doubted my popularity amongst my peers, as I had been the target of derision on many occasions. Having a mother who sent her child to school with notes that read "Please excuse Asha-lee from sport today as her aura is fragile" made me a sitting duck. A rather insensitive teacher announced this excuse to the class, enabling my detractors to have one more reason to chant the usual non-melodic phrase, "Asha-lee, Asha-lee, who is she? Asha-lee, Asha-lee, even she, has to pee!"

I arrived home in tears. Lalita lovingly cradled me in her arms and offered to make it better with a special herbal tea and a lavender-infused balm to rub into my throbbing head. This made me fling her arms aside and run to my bedroom, where more tears drowned my pillow.

The opportunity to see Lalita's curious world firsthand was probably the drawcard for the invited children. I didn't care. I was delighted and eagerly crossed the preceding days off my calendar.

On the appointed day, I tried to make our home normal. As fast as my mother placed candles and quaint dishes of oils around the room, I removed them.

'For goodness' sake, child, how can we improve their beings if we leave things as they are?'

I snatched a bunch of sage from her hand. 'Can't we just have it like everyone else's for one day?'

'Honey, I want what's best for you. The sage will be so cleansing.'

In the end, I gave up and let her decorate the place as if expecting the local misfits instead of being a party for ten-year-old girls.

While most children have party games like Pass the Parcel and Musical Chairs, my mother made impressionable youngsters sit through a lesson on the meaning of life as she dipped various oils from numerous bottles and dabbed them on the foreheads of their mesmerised faces. They soaked up her instructions on how they should meditate to add power to their physical essence.

An unscrupulous duo, otherwise known as my best friends, egged on the innocent girls. The scene would have presented a hilarious picture to an outsider. Three girls were chanting with serious intent, while two others were peeking out of their half-closed lids to check on the others. The local butcher's daughter sat with arms folded, frowning, declaring it was all a load of nonsense and she would rather have something to eat. The episode finished when Bella poked one of the more serious meditating pupils, causing her to scream, which made all guests either add their voice to the screaming or fall about laughing.

When Lalita gained control of the noisy

bunch and offered to read their palms, I scrambled from the room and brought back cold drinks of orange and peppermint. The accompanying food distracted them long enough to calm even the most sensitive members on the guest list. However, my nerves were on full alert, and my brain recorded a message promising never to again have a birthday party run by my mother.

Parting gifts of individually chosen incense sticks helped most of the entranced guests leave happily. A couple sulked after receiving carrot and celery sticks instead of the usual bag of treats. Lalita wasn't concerned about my embarrassment, patting them on the head and adding that carrot was good for their eyes. I could imagine the young girls' parents scolding them when they tried lighting the perfumed sticks while wondering at the strange world that was my home.

I hated all the chanting, all the blessing and the constant need to cleanse the soul. The ongoing changing aroma often gave me a headache, but I didn't dare complain; that would just bring on a specialised assault in an attempt to drive the demons from my brow.

My early teens passed slowly as I refused to be drawn on her magic carpet ride. By the time I turned seventeen, I believed in nothing. I didn't want to achieve harmony with the universe. I refused to accept we could contact the dead and repeatedly offered the opinion that my mother was insane.

Four

C andy and Bella arrived with flowers and chocolates. They finished a tour of my new home and didn't hesitate to point out the obvious.

'Small!'

'Old!'

'You can see right down the main street from your bedroom.'

'And up the side street from the bathroom.'

'Better keep the curtain closed.'

We listened to music echoing around the sparsely furnished room from a small radio balancing on the wobbly table next to the second-hand couch.

'Was your mum really cross?' Bella asked as she switched on the kettle.

'Well, she's been burning marigold and nettles all week.'

'And?'

'That means she is convinced I will become a tramp and resort to robbing a bank within the first week of my new existence.'

'Surely not!' Candy said.

I smirked, not at all surprised Candy believed my sarcasm. 'No, but she wasn't impressed. Anyway, I want to forget all that stuff. Honestly! What good has it done her?' I tapped the radio to encourage it to continue. 'I think she's trying to make herself believe in all that crap. How can anyone think the dead can talk, and even if they can, why would they choose her? "The Gift" she calls it. The Gift! Who needs it? Talking to dead people? Certainly not me!'

Bella shook her head and chose not to answer. She'd witnessed my rantings about my mother countless times. Candy was usually keener to delve where I didn't want her to go, but on this occasion, she thought better of it.

'Has she seen this place?' Candy asked.

'Not yet. I won't let her unless she promises not to bring her lotions and potions.'

'Wouldn't hurt, would it?' Bella carried a tray with three hot drinks and placed it on the floor.

'Not really, but I have to make a stand. This is my home, not her palace of dreams.'

It took us half an hour to finish our hot drinks and decide to get off our lazy bottoms. Then it took only fifteen minutes to unpack the boxes, placing my clothes in the only bedroom wardrobe and the few remaining household items in the small kitchen. With only bathroom and laundry items to dispense with, I wandered through to the bathroom and placed a basket of items next to the bath. When considering where all the paraphernalia could go, I was surprised to find a large cardboard box taking up most of the space on top of the dryer and called my friends to help remove it. We pushed aside the empty cartons on the rug and sat around the mysterious box.

'I wonder who it belonged to?' I pondered.

'Perhaps there's something valuable in it.'

'Mmm… mysterious,' Candy said.

'Maybe we'll find something interesting.'

'Just let me open the damn thing and find out,' I said.

'Hardly valuable,' Bella said as she hoisted out a belt.

'A scarf. Handmade by the looks of it.'

'Jolly nice, though.'

'What's that?'

'It's a wooden truck.'

'Child's toy?' Candy asked.

'Tiny.'

'Yep.'

'Anything else?'

There was nothing else remotely as exciting as the unopened box. Along with the attractive scarf and toy, there was the black leather belt with a bold buckle, a broken string of beads, several books and an empty jewellery box that had seen better days. We didn't bother with the uninteresting lump of material at the bottom.

Candy and Bella announced they had experienced enough excitement for the day, and it was time to go back to their boring lives. It didn't take a crystal ball to work out they were being sarcastic. However, I let them go, turned on my one indulgent purchase for my new home and settled down to watch the telly.

Five

The following day, I gave in and rang my mum, inviting her down to visit. A mere two kilometres separated us, and she didn't take long to arrive, bringing gifts of food. My favourite vegetarian casserole and homemade biscuits certainly resolved any coolness between us.

She too, noticed the lack of exciting views from the window and dropped the curtain from her hand with resignation. 'Pity you can't see the park,' she said.

'Yes, but I won't really be spending much time here. What with work and my social life, I'll really only be sleeping here.'

'It would've been much cheaper to sleep in your own bed at home.'

'Don't start. I'm twenty, old enough to be on my own.'

She took my hand and rubbed her thumb up and down my palm. 'But I miss you. I miss us chanting together. It's not the same on my own.'

I paused before pulling my hand away and shoving it in my pocket. 'I thought you understood I don't want to do that stuff anymore. I've tried to explain.'

'Yes, honey, I know.' She touched my shoulder. 'But you have been bestowed a gift, and you should expand your ability.'

I brushed her hand away. 'There isn't such a thing. And even if there is, I don't want it. I definitely do not intend to contribute to all that hocus-pocus. I really wish you could understand.'

Her forehead furrowed. Her hand went to her chin. 'I am sure you could be one of the few, if only you would try.'

'Mother! Stop talking about it.' I wanted to scream the rest of my annoyance but asked quietly, 'You want to see the rest of the place?'

That took no time, and I resorted to showing her the box of unclaimed items we'd found. Lalita caressed each item slowly and deliberately, annoying me in the process.

'They're just old stuff left behind, not items for a forensic team.'

'Sometimes, one can get vibes from persons who have passed over. They might've been left here for you... for a particular reason. We should meditate on them.'

Grabbing the scarf from her, I said, 'Don't start that again. Please. Don't make this into something it's not.' I tossed the scarf back in the box and left the other items where they were. Standing, I kicked the box under the table and asked, 'Can I get you some tea?'

We spent the rest of the visit pleasantly enough, and later I walked her to the bus stop. As we said our goodbyes, I hugged her with honest care for the person who had brought me life.

Six

On arriving home, I ran into Mr Nelli—this shortened version was his choice, not mine—and asked him about the items scattered over my couch.

'I not know who they belong. Many people come and go.'

'What should I do with them?'

His teeth did a little dance as he pulled on his ear. 'Let me look. I come now.'

I wanted to clutch his arm and help him up the stairs but left him to painstakingly climb each step as his breath rushed out noisily, like an old train building up steam. Finally, we reached my door, and I ushered him in.

'You are moved in,' he said unnecessarily. 'It's nice.'

'Thanks. Here's the box. Look at these things. Are they likely to be needed by anyone?'

He glanced at the items on the couch and turned his attention to the box. He rummaged through a couple of undisturbed items on the bottom and found a minute photo.

'So old. It is a bambino,' and he tossed it back into the box. 'You can keep. Maybe throw out.'

'I like the scarf. I might keep it.'

'Okay, you keep. No one to mind. They even might be from before they make the changes to the big house.'

'Changes? You mean making them into units. They're not that old, are they?'

'I not remember. When I be first married–is about the time of all the building. I might have some stories at home. I did keep newspapers. Many people live here. Never mind, I look for you.' He scratched at his chin and walked towards the door. 'The old pieces, they should have been thrown away before. You can do it. Or you keep. It is for you to make decision. Good day, Miss.'

While I sifted through the information of his departing chatter, he sucked at his teeth, moved away, and closed the door.

I sorted through the items, deciding to keep the belt, scarf and little wooden truck. I stuffed the other bits back into the box and unceremoniously pushed it into the bottom of the kitchen pantry behind the esky and insect repellent.

One week later, I summoned enough courage to

visit my mother. I dressed carefully, trying to avoid anything which might bring about the need for cleansing or other spiritualistic encounters. At the last minute, I picked up the wooden truck. It looked homemade, and I could use it to sidetrack any unwanted discussions. I dropped it into my bag and headed for the bus stop just around the corner, taking a seat on the bench and armed with a book.

Looking up from my book, I sensed a person next to me. She smiled a greeting and I returned it, glancing down into the pram she was rocking.

'Boy or girl?' I asked to prevent stumbling for a gender.

'He's a boy. Kenny.'

The glow covering her face showed me she was the mother. Compelled to continue the conversation, I placed a bookmark in the outstretched pages and closed the book.

'Are you waiting for the bus too?' I asked.

'No, just enjoying a break before I walk home again.'

'Do you have far to go?'

'Just up the street and around the corner.' She straightened her cardigan. 'I'm not in a hurry. I hate being on my own, and the sunshine is lovely today.'

I nodded. 'He's sleeping well.'

'Yes. Kenny's a good baby, and the pram is comfortable.'

I'd noticed the pram with my first glance. It wasn't one of these jogging-stroller contraptions all the young mothers push as they hurry along, dressed in their aerobic outfits trying to return to the pre-baby figure as quickly as celebrities in magazines. Kenny's was made of vinyl with enough room for a sleeping toddler to stretch out. The hood provided adequate shade, and I could see it had the option to fold back. The young mother was dressed in a skirt and twinset, and the whole picture didn't seem quite right somehow. Probably a retro freak, I thought. It's big right now.

I wasn't sure whether I should open my book again or extend the conversation. However, options became obsolete when she started crying.

'Oh, are you okay?' I said, as one does when confronted with tears, even though one obviously isn't alright when you're crying while sitting at a bus stop on a perfectly lovely day. Nevertheless, I did ask and promptly forgot about my book.

'I'm sorry,' she wailed, 'I didn't mean to do this, but lately I've been crying rather a lot.'

'What's up?'

'I'm so worried. My husband hasn't been

home for weeks, and I can't get in touch with him.'

'No mobile?'

Her mouth tried unsuccessfully to smile. 'We moved from the country when the farm couldn't support us anymore. His brother has a wife and three children. The income was barely enough to cover their needs. They said we were young and could manage on our own.

'We came here, and Oscar found a job in a factory.' She paused and looked at me as she sniffed. 'Oscar's my husband.'

'Oh, right.' I thought of the agate Lalita had for inducing luck in one's life. I forced the intrusive thought away. 'That's good.'

'It was *great*.'

With the ominous emphasis, I knew the story would take a turn at some point.

'Oscar found a lovely little place in town, and we made some nice friends. We were so proud of ourselves. We were even saving for our own home.' She shrugged and smiled meekly. 'I managed to get a part-time job at a café up the street. Things were going so well. I even made some curtains. You should have seen my husband's face when he came home that night. He danced me around and told me our home was as pretty as I was. The curtains hid the ugly blinds and made the place so cheerful, so the next payday, I bought a remnant from the local haberdashery and made some cushion covers. We were so happy.' She pulled the pram closer.

'On the weekends, we'd walk down by the river. He always held my hand. We'd have a picnic and paddle our feet in the cold water. Neither of us went right in because we couldn't swim, you know, coming from the country. Never got the chance to learn. Too much dry land and always work to be done.'

By now, she had wiped away the tears with an embroidered handkerchief she'd found amongst the oddments at the end of the baby's feet. That was another thing; how many crochet rugs are in use these days?

The rug-of-many-colours formed a cocoon around baby Kenny, who was oblivious to the choice made by his doting out-of-date mother.

'I don't know what to do. Should I go after him, or should I just wait? Waiting is so hard, isn't it?'

'Certainly is. This bus seems to be taking forever.'

'If I go to the city, what will I find? He didn't really want to go, you know. He only left because we'd spent nearly all our savings. The job here was a good one. The company had been there for over fifty years. We thought we were set for life.'

The tears started again, and I couldn't fathom what to say.

'"Losing your job once is bad enough; a second time is just careless." That's what he used to say.' Her forced chuckle disappeared when she said, 'It was supposed to be a joke. After a while, it wasn't. He was so disillusioned. First the farm, then the factory. They lost a big order and had to cut back. Not his fault, but he felt he'd let me down. I couldn't make him see sense. We had my meagre wages, and I talked the café owner into giving me more hours, but it didn't solve everything. Oscar felt like less of a man with his wife earning the money. I tried to make him see it was only temporary. I really tried.'

The sudden silence made me uncomfortable. I hadn't been exposed to many of life's hardships and disappointments. My sympathy could only come from a caring heart, not from experience. As I made benign noises to project my thoughts, she continued her story.

'Then I fell pregnant. At first, we were so happy. It lifted Oscar's mood, and he started looking for work again. Walking up and down all the back streets, almost begging for a job. We sat together and tried to make plans, but I suffered from morning sickness. It was horrid. I lost my job because they needed someone more reliable. We had no money coming in. Our savings dwindled. We cried such a lot. What could we do?'

I shrugged and tried to look comforting. 'Welfare?'

'Now he doesn't come home from his new job in the city. He used to. We agreed, every second weekend—without fail. It was wonderful. It was as if we were dating all over again. I would sleep with curlers in my hair so it would be nice, and I always put on my best dress. After a while, some of them wouldn't fit. I had to let most of my skirts out as I couldn't afford maternity clothes.' She ran her pale hands over her stomach as if remembering the special time. 'Not like my workmate. Her husband made her finish up as soon as she knew she was expecting. And so many gorgeous clothes. Those smocks she had! Probably had three or four of those special maternity trousers as well. Not me. I wore my dresses over my slacks and had to hold them together with safety pins. Never mind. I was happy.

'Finally, Oscar got a job in the city. It paid well. He said he liked it, but now I'm not sure. Doesn't really talk about it much. Said, "a job is a job," and it was good money. We're saving again. Maybe he will come home this weekend. I hope so. Kenny misses his daddy.'

Kenny was missing many things as he was

still asleep, tucked beneath the garish covers. I thought of the toy in my bag and wondered if this young mother would like it. As I picked it out of my bag, I lost the grip of my book, and everything tumbled to the ground. Retrieving the book and then the toy, I turned to offer it to her, but there was no one beside me. I stood up quickly, and once again, scattered things at my feet.

'Damn! Where did she go?'

There was no trace of her despite me walking a dozen or more paces in both directions. Fortunately, the bus's arrival saved the effort of solving that particular problem at that precise moment.

Seven

I arrived at my mother's and explained as best I could. 'Disappeared. Gone. Poof!'

'Odd, very odd!'

'Not helpful. Not very helpful, Lalita.'

'Let's see.' Lalita frowned at me. 'You say she was dressed in a different manner.'

'Yeah. Retro. Sort of.'

'Mmm... You said they were from a farm originally.'

'Yes'

'A crocheted baby's cover?'

'Yes.'

'Not so odd after all.'

'Really?'

My mother's initial response amazed me. She could turn a morning tea party into a séance run by the devil, but here she was downplaying this curious event.

'Perhaps she's just a country girl with old-fashioned clothes. She said they didn't have much money. Maybe the clothes were from second-hand shops.'

'I just feel there was something else, but I can't put my finger on it.' I ran my finger around the rim of the cup on my lap. 'I mean, how did she disappear so quickly?'

'Perhaps it wasn't as quickly as you thought. You did say you had everything all over the footpath.'

'I did, but it was really just my book and the toy.'

'Well then, you're either such a butterfingers that you didn't see her go—' Lalita nodded, picking up an unlit candle from the coffee table, 'or she disappeared in a puff of the hereafter.' She leaned against my shoulder. 'Maybe we should look at that possibility.'

Ah! I thought, here we go. Why did I tell her? I should've known better.

Lalita was just getting started, but I needed to clear my head of this encounter. As it was, we were sitting over cups of wild daisy tea. After a moment's quietness, my mother reached over and covered my hand with hers.

'It's possible.'

I raised my eyes and looked at her. My mood

was sombre, and I tried to convey the need to end this conversation.

'Well,' she said, 'you did ask me what I thought.'

'I know.' I leaned forward and placed the cup on the table. 'But now I think I would rather forget about it.'

'You can't.' She squeezed my hand. 'If someone needs your help, you need to be there for them.'

I pulled my hand away, stood and pouted, 'But she disappeared!'

'Yes, but she may return.'

That thought hadn't reached my brain until then. I squinted at my mother, trying to convince myself of her suggested interpretation. 'Lalita, it's interesting, but I am sure there is a perfectly good explanation without making it into a production from Ghost Story.'

'We'll see, shall we?' She stood and placed her hand on my arm. 'Now, do you want some of that leek pie I made or not?'

Eight

A few days later, Bella and Candy were to arrive on the eleven-twenty train. We'd planned to have lunch at the quaint café two blocks up from my flat. They served plain fare but inexpensive and plentiful, and Bella had tried to convince us the iced chocolates were worth the extra exercise needed to counteract the calories.

I waited on the platform, leaning against the brick wall surrounding the newsagency. Trains rushed through, taking people to their destinations.

Suddenly a man ran past, calling, 'Wait! Wait! Oh, damnation! Wait!'

Not entirely unusual at a minor train station, but the trains on this line ran every few minutes. I stretched taller to see if he caught his train, but there were other commuters blocking my view.

Not long after, my friends arrived, full of chatter, eager to impart every detail of our separated time. I butted into their conversation, 'Did you see if that man caught his train?'

'What man?'

'The one with the hat.'

'What hat?'

'It's called a fedora,' I said.

'A fed... what?'

I could tell Bella wasn't interested in the detail I had learned from my smartphone. 'Doesn't matter. Did you see if he caught the train?'

'Nup. Who was he?'

'No one, really. He was yelling and seemed frantic to catch that particular train. You didn't see him then?'

Candy chuckled. 'Plenty of blokes with caps. No one with a hat.'

'Too many people,' Bella added. She changed the subject while I watched the train pull out, hoping to catch a glimpse of a hat inside the carriage. 'How's the flat?'

'Good.'

'Just good?'

I forced myself to consider Bella's question. 'Well... great. I guess.'

'I thought you'd be over the moon,' Candy said. 'I mean, you were really angry that day, wanting to leave Lalita and everything.'

'Mmm… I was. I've calmed down a bit since then.'

'So, you're sorry you moved?'

Not completely engaged in the conversation, my mind still being committed to the man in the hat, I replied half-heartedly, 'No, not at all.'

'You sure? I thought you'd be a little more excited about it all.'

I stopped walking. Pushing aside the nonsense of a late commuter, I focused on Bella's probing. 'I needed to get my own place. Yes, I was angry. Do I regret it? No way.'

Candy rolled her eyes. 'Come on you two, I'm hungry. Let's get going,' We linked arms and moved towards our destination.

'Nice belt.'

'Thanks,' I said. 'It's the one from the box.'

'Oh! That one. Awesome.'

'They say if you keep something long enough, it'll come back into fashion,' Candy added.

'Well, it has,' I said.

Once seated in the café, we spent time exchanging stories, laughing a lot. I asked if either of them wanted to come with me to a book club.

'Nup,' Candy said. 'Can't think of anything worse. Mum goes to one. She panics if she doesn't finish the obligatory book in time.'

'Why a book club?' Bella asked.

'I saw it in the local paper. It's either that or yoga.'

'Yoga! You didn't want to join when I went last year.' Candy fake-punched my arm. 'You said it was too much like meditating.'

Picking at my sandwich, my prolonged sigh exaggerated my reluctance to expand. 'I'm trying to do something in my spare time Lalita wouldn't approve of.' I picked out the tomato from my sandwich. 'Does that make me sound pathetic?'

Bella and Candy exchanged a subtle glance and shrugged in unison.

'Look, you might think I'm mad,' my snort made them smile, 'but you know what she's like, and I want to be different. Finally, I get to do stuff my mother doesn't even have to know about.'

'Yeah, right,' Bella said. 'Whatever you decide, you'll tell her.'

'No, I won't.' I thought about how Lalita and I had survived together. Yes, in a world of make-believe most of the time, but her support was guaranteed. 'Yeah, maybe I will, but afterwards.'

'So, it's yoga or a book club... hardly mind-blowing.'

'Any better ideas then?' I slurped up the last of the milkshake.

'A place where good-looking fellows go,' Candy suggested.

'The pub?' Bella grinned.

'Does Asha have a better idea?' Candy grinned back at Bella.

'Nup, the pub sounds good. The one in Parker's Lane has a terrific band on Saturdays.'

'I'm up for it,' Candy said.

'Me too,' I said, thinking about what I could wear.

We made plans to meet at Candy's flat before checking out Parker's Ale House on the following Saturday evening.

I returned home, happy in my solitude, glad of my own space, and spent the evening on my one-and-only couch reading a novel of doubtful originality. My mother would have been appalled. She frowned on books of this nature and deemed them inappropriate for the growing soul. I was tired of looking after my soul. Well, that was only partly true. I didn't want to actually damage my soul, but I did want to experience ordinary things like reading trashy, old-fashioned novels.

I'd found the dog-eared version I had in my hand on the bottom shelf of the bedroom wardrobe. Jim was in love with Deborah, who hated him and lusted after Warren. Phillip didn't want anything to do with Jayne while Jayne was trying to annoy Deborah enough to make her leave so she could have Jim. What a plot! Who knows how old the book was, but I was pleased to be doing such an ordinary thing.

Things were never ordinary in my mother's home.

When I was seven, Lalita decided she would contact my grandmother. This appealed to me as I was jealous of Bella's bond with her grandmother, even though I shared many visits with them.

However, my grandmother was dead. I knew this, but living in the house with Lalita, I didn't question how this was a disadvantage.

I put on my violet dress that matched Lalita's, as I'd been taught. This enabled us to connect with higher energies and spiritual realms; a necessity when one couldn't use the telephone to contact one's relatives.

We sat: Mother chanting an ancient ritual; daughter humming along in a singsong fashion. Lalita spent twenty minutes clasping blue lace agate to enhance communication. Pink candles wafted their scent in our direction, reflecting love, harmony and family into our beings.

I wriggled impatiently on the meditation cushion for the last ten excruciating minutes. In between the chants, Lalita growled at me to stop fidgeting. Up until then, I wondered what would happen if the "departed" actually talked to us.

Then, when I mentioned I felt a presence, Lalita started yelling. 'Oh, my goodness, my goodness, child. Where? What happened? Tell me... tell me about it.'

Her hysterics surprised me. 'Just felt like someone was there.'

'Who was it? What did they look like?'

'I couldn't tell, but it could've been Grandma Rosie.'

Her arms flapped, reminding me of seagulls. She forced me up from the cushion, hugging and then releasing me so quickly that I stumbled.

'What did she say? What did she say to you?'

'I didn't understand her.' I realised her interrogations weren't going to end in a hurry. 'I... I don't know.'

'Don't be so dismissive. You have to tell me.' She grabbed my shoulders. 'How did you do it? Tell me, child.'

My mystical mother, who spent hours calming everything from lost souls to the universe, yelled at me because I was missing my true calling and denying the very results of her teachings for which she had worked so hard.

Determined to communicate with Rosie again, Lalita forced me to participate in a ritual every day for two weeks. I missed school, and when I returned, suffered further embarrassment as the teacher read aloud an abbreviated version of my mother's note. This humiliated me even more than the scolding I received from Lalita for not producing a message from beyond.

From that time on, whenever Lalita forced me to wear my violet dress and sit on the purple meditation cushion, I screwed up my eyes tightly and prayed for them to go away. I hoped my requests would counteract hers, and any hovering departed folk would leave me alone.

Nine

Bella phoned for a quick gossip about Candy's new boyfriend. I grinned, remembering how quickly Jack had passed into oblivion without Candy requiring any help from the essence of "whatever". Apparently, Travis was not quite tall, dark and handsome, but cool enough to make a young woman's heart flutter. After being informed of all the gossip from Bella, I settled down amongst the cushions on my couch and rang Candy with the express purpose of hearing it all again.

'He's so lovely,' she started out.

'Mmm... where have I heard that before?'

'Don't be like that Asha-lee. Jack was okay, but this one's the real deal.'

'Real deal, eh! That I have to see.'

'Exactly.' Her voice sounded out her intentional but oblique request.

'What?' A tingle shot across my forehead. 'No, Candy. "Exactly" nothing!'

'I want you to meet him, of course.'

Here we go, I thought, and waited.

'Um, Asha... I'd like... He has to get your approval.'

I held my mobile away from my ear and shook my head. After hearing Candy's raised voice and knowing exactly what her half-asked request implied, I said slowly and deliberately, 'No. He does not. And I won't.'

'Asha, pleeease! Just for me,' she begged.

Again, I waited.

'Look, I promise it'll be the last time. Come on, pleeease,' she begged again. Her voice altered, coming through in a demanding tone, 'I have to make sure he has a decent aura.'

'Candice!' I elbowed a cushion to the floor.

'Well, what's the point of having a friend who can see an aura if she doesn't put it to good use?'

'I'm trying to forget all that stuff. Anyway, I don't think I can anymore. Haven't for ages.'

Well, not that I would admit. I refused to be drawn into any psychic possibilities. It was possible for me to see people's aura, but I didn't want to. I didn't want to be the scary person who did weird stuff. That was Lalita—not me. I hate being different. Why is it I can see auras around the people sitting opposite on the train? It's embarrassing coming face to face with one's boss, who is wearing a decidedly romantic aura after returning from a meeting with a client.

I came back to the present and agreed to meet the wonderful new boyfriend as long as I wasn't expected to "perform".

'Alright then,' Candy agreed reluctantly.

I wasn't convinced but asked, 'When, and where?'

'Soon. At Donny's café.'

Soon came around quickly, and I headed for Donny's café, a favourite hangout for the young and trendy. I was young but never considered trendy, so I made an extra effort when choosing my outfit. Jeans, crisp white shirt and high-heeled boots, along with the newly acquired belt and some wooden beads. The outfit brought me closer to being modern but hardly trendy. Never mind, I wasn't likely to be the centre of attention, and it was the best I could do.

At the train station, the timetable announced I had seven minutes to wait. I stood, once again, leaning against the building, watching the throngs as they ebbed and flowed from carriages. A hat caught my eye, and I remembered the young man who had been in a hurry to catch the train the last time I was here. The familiar wearer of the hat came towards me, glanced in my direction, but moved on. A few minutes later, he returned and, like in an old movie, removed his hat before asking if I knew which bus went to

Redhill Road.

'I usually walk, but I'm late,' he said.

'You can get a bus from outside the station. Up closer to Main Street.' I pointed out of the station. 'Look for number 26.'

He hesitated, and I caught a glimpse of pain in his eyes as he passed his fingers through the hair on his hatless head.

'Are you okay?' I asked.

'Sort of. Difficult time. Have to go. Thank you for the information.'

He replaced his hat and strode off into the moving crowd. I could see his hat above the other heads as they left the platform.

I arrived at Donny's first and didn't have to wait long before Candy and Bella arrived looking super cool. I really should make an effort to buy something new.

'Where's the boyfriend?' I asked, looking for an eligible male amongst the predominately female customers.

'He's coming later. Said he would give us time to talk about him first.'

My eyes widened. 'Did he really?'

'Yep.' She smirked, pleased at my reaction. 'He has two older sisters and reckons he knows how we like to talk about our boyfriends.'

'That's a healthy ego.' I frowned, wondering if I could even dent her enthusiasm with a bad reading of his aura. 'Anyway,' I said, 'let's get something to drink first.'

We'd exhausted every single attribute of Travis just before he fronted up. On our second round of hot drinks, this time without a cake, an anxious Candy introduced us. I must say he was rather cute. He certainly charmed us, telling us how lovely we all looked.

He sat for a while, asking us questions I'm sure Candy had provided. After another five minutes, he kissed Candy on the mouth, told her he'd ring later and left.

'What do you think?' Candy urged before he was even out of earshot.

'More than nice,' Bella said.

'Rather good looking,' I offered.

'Yes, but what do you think of him, Asha?'

'Hardly a long chat, but, yeah, he seems okay.'

Candy pushed my arm. 'Asha?'

I leaned away from her and pretended not to understand. 'Seems lovely. How did you meet him?'

'Don't change the subject,' she growled. 'What about his aura?'

'I told you. I don't do that anymore. Anyway,

you promised.'

'No, I didn't. I said after this one.'

I knew she'd get around my protests, but I tried again. 'I wish you wouldn't ask. I really don't want to.'

Bella was no help at all. She raised her eyebrows and smirked. 'But you can.'

'Not always.'

'What did you see?' Candy leaned forward, almost knocking over a mug. 'Please tell me. He seems a bit too good to be true. I need some validation.'

'I can't, Candy.' I pulled my seat closer to the table and feigned an interest in the dirty dishes.

Snatching away the wrinkled serviette from my hand, she said in a demanding voice, 'I know you can. I was there that day.' She looked at Bella for backup. 'We both were.' Touching my hand, she said, 'Just this time. Pleeease.'

I didn't want my best friend begging in a public place. I knew what she was talking about. I too, remembered the first time I realised I could see an aura.

Bella lived three houses up from our place, and with Candy living over my back fence, we made a formidable trio in the neighbourhood. We were always up to something. Nothing particularly bad, just typical schoolgirl mischief. We would pinch flowers from one neighbour's garden and leave them on the doorstep of another house, ring the doorbell and bolt.

We drew toothpaste faces on glass panels. Smiley faces on the windows of people we liked, and a great big miserable face on Mr Britten's front door. He was always growling at the local kids, and this was our form of revenge.

Sleepovers happened almost every weekend, as we couldn't stand to be apart. Good thing mobile phones weren't available; the batteries would've run flat in no time.

During high school, we often did our homework together—that was the plausible excuse for staying up late—punctuated by a lot of giggling.

Bella and Candy always wanted to stay over at my house. Lalita didn't place many constraints on us, and the likelihood of the weird and wonderful enticed them. I would argue it wasn't my turn, but with two against one, I never had a chance.

It was on one of these occasions I commented on the coloured shapes hovering around our heads. We were standing in front of Lalita's large mirror, admiring our attempts at applying make-up. Heavy eyeliner over cheap false eyelashes, thickly applied green eyeshadow and lipstick in garish colours distorted our teenage faces. Lalita was to judge our attempts, and the winner would receive the first choice in a treat for supper.

As the other two fought over space in the mirror, I stood back feeling a little tired and drowsy. I didn't need to win, as all the so-called treats weren't new to me.

The images in the mirror were amazing. Three young faces all painted within an inch of hilarity. Surrounding them, in a halo-shaped form, were more glowing colours. I stared for a moment or two before asking, 'Can you see them?'

'See what?'

'The halos.'

'Halos?' Candy squeaked; Bella whispered.

'Well, I suppose they are auras, really.'

'Wow, where?' Bella almost fell into the washbasin as she leaned forward.

I blinked, and the apparitions faded into the mirror without a trace.

I didn't want to say anything to my mother, but my friends built the moment into an event worthy of a full orchestra with an obligatory drum roll.

Lalita refused to give a verdict on our make-up attempts until I told her everything I'd seen. The colours, the size of each colour, if they moved, if they blended. My mother skipped between us, repeating her questions, touching our faces, smiling, chuckling, repeating to me, 'I knew you could do it.'

When I stuttered and stammered, unwilling to give her details, she gripped my shoulders and demanded I concentrate. 'Tell me. Explain, child.'

I could smell the peppermint on her breath as she put her hands on my cheeks and forced me to look at her.

Recalling the episode when my grandmother spoke to me, I realised if I didn't give Lalita what she wanted, her pleadings would never stop.

I made things up. When she smiled, I painted a bigger picture. When she folded her arms and glared at me with disbelief, I altered the description.

'Oh! Maybe not blue going into the yellow. Perhaps it was the other way.' That sort of thing. Finally, she stopped demanding answers.

However, it wasn't the last I heard of auras.

Candy won the make-up competition, and I lost my sanity. They wouldn't stop talking about my ability to see something they couldn't. They wanted to know what it meant for them to have the colours I'd described. They didn't know I'd made up most of it, simply because I couldn't really remember the exact details and because I was a little scared.

First, Grandmother muttered from the grave, and now I could see auras. My stomach echoed my rebellion; I felt sick most of the time. I just wanted to be normal. Was I ever going to be just like everyone else?

After this first episode, Lalita suddenly had a myriad of books on reading auras, and she expected me to study right through to the last page of the six volumes. My friends constantly asked about their auras, and I would occasionally oblige. In the right atmosphere, auras are revealed, but mostly I told them what I thought they wanted to hear. Sure, I was interested to a point. I didn't want to be weird, but I wondered if there was something for me to learn from it all.

Once, I told my mother's plump friend her aura was developing a brownish tinge—the colour of gluttony, and she should be careful about what she ate. Well! She grabbed my t-shirt and wiggled it back and forth while she told me I was "the devil" and my mother should learn how to control me.

I certainly learned from that. I learned not to tell people what they didn't want to hear.

So, having my friend beg me to explain her new boyfriend's aura made me very wary. If I told her the truth—that I hadn't witnessed anything—she wouldn't believe me. In the end,

I expressed a generic opinion that all his colours were where they should be. 'Go for it, girl,' I added for good measure and hoped she would stop pressing.

After finishing our drinks, we browsed the shops and promised to go shopping together next week. I headed home, pleased to have spent time with my friends.

Ten

The mornings had turned cold, and after I'd dressed in jeans and a jumper, I added the scarf that lay on my couch where I'd left it. It looked hand-knitted with bands of blue, brown and beige. I thought it rather glamorous, and it suited my nutmeg-coloured coat.

After finding my ever-missing keys, I opened the front door, and as I prepared to exit, a man rushed into my lounge room yelling out for Josie.

After recovering from the shock of his unexpected entrance, I yelled back, 'Excuse me, if you don't mind!'

'Where's Jocelyn?' He turned and glared at me.

'No one here by that name. Can you please leave?'

'I'm not leaving. Where's my daughter?'

Standing with one hand on my hip and the other pointing out the doorway, I spoke in the sternest voice I could muster, 'Sir, I have no idea who you are talking about, but I can assure you there is no one else here.'

He stopped striding and looked me up and down. 'And who are you?'

'Never mind who I am, who are you and what are you doing yelling for your daughter in my place?'

'I've come for Josie. We have to find her and the baby.'

My voice turned high-pitched. 'And a baby?' I remembered Kenny. What is it with me and babies?

This stranger peered into the bedroom and bathroom as if I was hiding the person called Josie. My stomach constricted, my hands trembled. A lunatic was loose in my place. I had to get rid of him

'You can see she isn't here. You've obviously come to the wrong place.' I pointed out the door again. 'I would like you to leave NOW.'

He stepped towards the door, continuing to look around. 'This is the corner of Redhill Road, isn't it?'

'Yes. So?'

'I'm not in the wrong place then.'

'Well, doesn't matter, I still want you to leave.'

My temperature rose from anxiety and being overdressed, so I removed my coat and scarf and tossed them at a chair. When I turned back, he had, thankfully, gone.

I needed a hot cup of tea and only avoided having an anxiety attack when realising I was late. Lalita wouldn't be pleased if the prepared lunch was spoilt. Making do with some choc milk Candy had left in the fridge—I found it neither calming nor satisfying—I grabbed my coat, locked the door and ran down the stairs.

Arriving at the place which had been my home for twenty years made me nostalgic. I hugged Lalita and squinted hard to stop the sentimental tears from being more than bubbles in the back of my eyes.

My old room looked tidy without the damning evidence of my occupation, and I spent a few minutes smiling while looking at the blue walls, the sheer lime-green curtains and the numerous cosmic pictures that had been a reluctant part of my previous life.

Why had I agreed to live like this? Was the power of my mother's mind really so strong I bent to her every wish, or was it a matter of keeping the peace the easy way?

Lalita was convinced one could heal with aromatherapy, bring peace with candles and chant your way to a better being. All this hocus-pocus scared me a little, if I was honest. I'd been surrounded by her teachings from the start of life, but as each year passed, I sensed her longing to have these notions a fact rather than really believing it possible. I saw no evidence of her success. Admittedly, one felt different after a twenty-minute meditation session surrounded by smouldering candles whose aroma pleased the scent buds. I've now discovered the same is achievable with a glass or two of red wine, soothing music and a good book.

As far as I could see, being an alternative type gave her an identity. She was that crazy lady down the street. The person who others gossiped about. Lorna Underwood was ordinary, an individual you would pass in the street without turning around. Lorna wouldn't have raised an eyebrow or caused any gossip, but Lalita Anglesea? She's a different proposition. Lalita could wear statement outfits. She was the character who had dream catchers in every window, bunches of sweetgrass hanging at the front door to keep evil spirits away, and who welcomed you by offering to contact departed loved ones. One could never ignore a person like that.

I roamed through the house and joined my mother in the kitchen, dishing up delicious-smelling pumpkin and ginger soup. 'Mmm... smells good.'

'Thanks, honey. Homegrown. Did you see the patch out the back?'

'Not yet, must though.'

'How's the solo living going?'

'Good, good.' I nodded, trying to be convincing.

'Really?'

'Yep, I had choc milk.'

'Whatever for?' Lalita paused, ladle in mid-air.

'Just 'cos.'

'Did you like it?'

'No, not really.' I curled up my lip. 'It stuck to my teeth and made me cough.'

'Lactose.'

'Yep, probably.'

We both laughed. She laughed at me, knowing I was avoiding admitting her strict dietary teachings were good for me. I laughed to end the conversation.

I wanted to tell her about the strange people I'd been meeting but didn't know if I was able to cope with listening to her interpretation of the situation. I had my suspicions, but avoidance of reality seemed a good option from where I was standing, and "let sleeping dogs lie" came to mind.

'Are you looking after yourself?'

'Yes,' I replied softly.

'Do you need any incense?'

'No!'

'Just asking, that's all. Are you still having that dream?'

The silence filling the room caused my mother to stop cutting the bread and look around for an answer. 'Well?'

'I don't want to talk about it.'

'You never do.' She pointed the knife at me. 'Asha, you have to realise sometimes talking about things makes it easier.'

'And sometimes it doesn't.'

'So, you still see it.'

'Yes, if you really must know.' I pinched a piece of crust. 'The fan shape is still there. The tears still fall.'

'Your grandmother would have worked it out.'

'Well, she isn't here.' I walked away from the bench. 'It's just you and me, and you bloody well can have all the guesses in the world, and it still won't be solved.'

She placed the knife calmly on the bench. I knew I shouldn't have yelled at her, but I'd had enough. It always felt like an inquisition with Lalita. Everything had to have a meaning.

This recurring dream bothered me. Since I can remember, it's been the same. A shape resembling a fan or a flat shell, would float around my head then suddenly, pieces would fall out of it. I could only describe them as tears or dewdrops. I always woke with a sense of loss.

'I'm sorry I brought it up,' Lalita said. 'But when did it start again?'

'Just since I've been on my own.'

'Ah!'

'Ah what?' I raised my hands in exasperation. 'I suppose you think if I moved home, it would stop.' I stepped towards the doorway. 'Nothing ever stops it. The dream always comes back.'

'Maybe it's all that bother you've been having with that young mother.'

'Bother? Honestly, I've hardly thought about it.' I sighed. 'And, she hasn't returned.'

A strange feeling made me turn around. It was as if a crowd was pushing me forward, everyone nudging the person in front of them until they couldn't help but push against me. I followed Lalita to the table and shuddered as I sat down and accepted the bowl of soup.

'Maybe it's Rosie,' said Lalita as she placed her elbows on the table and leaned towards me. 'Maybe she's explaining something.'

'You mean the dream? Why would it be Rosie?' I asked. 'Can't it simply be a funny dream? Why does it have to be a dead person speaking to me?'

'Have you stopped to think about the people that only you can see?'

'Who? The man looking for Josie? I was the only one home. I'm sure others saw the man at the station.'

Lalita leaned further across the table. 'A man? Josie? You didn't tell me about them. I meant the mother with the pram and the ones when you were a kid.' She sat back and folded her arms. 'But now I want to hear about those other ones.'

I banged my spoon on the table and glared at my mother. 'Why would dead people want to speak to me? And why only these few?' I waved my arms around, inviting anyone floating around the room to come closer. Soup flicked onto the tablecloth. 'Come one, come all. Aren't there any other dead people who want to talk to me? Why only Rosie? Why random people? Let's have everyone talking. What about my father?' My anger started to fade, and I let my arms fall into my lap. 'Why doesn't he talk to me?'

'Asha, that's enough. Let's not fight. Eat something, and we'll talk about it later.'

'I'm done. Just let me be.'

'Well, eat up and look after your body at least, and then we'll think about your inner self.'

'My inner self is great. I'm just super tired, and you promised not to do that stuff.'

'I know I did, but you have such a natural talent for it.'

'It's nonsense, and I'd rather not talk about it.' I pouted like a six-year-old.

'You'll let me know if you need anything.'

'No!' Now I yelled like a teenager. 'I don't need incense... or candles... or any of that crap.'

She grinned at me. 'I meant food, or a chat.'

'Oh, sorry.' I was suitably chastened. 'Yes. Yes, I will.'

As we sipped the wonderful pumpkin soup, my eyes fell on a picture on the dresser of three generations. In my mother's favourite photo, my grandmother cradled me in her arms as my mother looked over her shoulder. Silver candles surrounded the picture frame, probably my mother's latest attempt to bring psychic power and lunar magic to me.

My grandmother passed over when I was four years old. Lalita constantly rabbited on how much alike we were. 'You have her long forehead. It means wisdom, you know. Look at your hair; it curls just like your grandmother's.'

I'd heard a myriad of stories about how

wonderful my mother's mother was and how proud Grandma Rosie was to have a granddaughter. Tears invariably accompanied the stories of my grandmother.

Today was no exception. I half-listened to the repeated story of my grandparent's struggle to buy a house during such economic distress. Then came the inevitable recounting of joy when I was born and the sadness of following events. Lalita reached out and touched my hand. 'My daughter.' She brushed away the moisture from her cheek with the back of her other hand.

I'd never worked out what she wanted me to say at moments like this. Did she want me to give buckets of praise for being a sole parent? Was I supposed to voice my approval of the way we lived? Different from the humdrum of the ordinary.

I put down my spoon and placed both my hands gently on hers. 'Yeah, thanks heaps, Lalita.'

She nodded but didn't smile, and after I pulled my hands away, she curled her long fingers together as if she was shaking hands with herself. I sighed audibly. 'Lalita, you're not alone. I'm only a few streets away. I have a mobile, for goodness' sake, if you need me.'

We ate the rest of our soup in silence. I struggled to breathe evenly. The spoon scraped on the bottom of the bowl as I ate quickly.

Between mouthfuls, I watched her. Would she never let go of me? Was I supposed to feel guilty? It was the first time she had so blatantly used the sign of seclusion in front of me. I'd been taught to use my inner strength as an advantage. Self-reliance. Confidence. All the platitudes given to me from as far back as I could remember. As my mother gripped her fingers in this particular manner, she was telling me she was alone.

I wanted to yell, 'Bullshit! Don't hang that on me,' but I finished my soup, told her how tasty it was, and went home where I too was alone, but not lonely.

Eleven

fter a week of text messages and phone calls, Candy, Bella and I finally arranged to go late night shopping together.

I reached an almost empty train station; it was the hiatus after the evening rush.

On approaching the platform, I spotted the strange young man I'd previously encountered. He sat with his suit jacket draped over his knee. His head sagged towards his chest. Bulky, rough-skinned fingers drooped between his knees. His eyes looked at nothing; his vision directed towards his feet. His fedora, which had initially brought him to my attention, balanced on his thigh. Compelled to talk to him, I walked slowly, unsure of what to say. He looked up, and his beautiful brown eyes showed anguish and despair.

'What's wrong?' I asked. 'Can I help at all?'

There was a flash of recognition before his tortured eyes dropped down again and his voice seeped out. 'It's my wife. It was a terrible visit.

She needs money, and I couldn't give her any. We argued. I couldn't tell her. I don't know what to do.'

I sat down next to him. 'Is there anything I can do?'

I could see his lips trembling and he breathed deeply, struggling to stop tears from forming. The fedora wobbled as he stretched his legs. I wanted to clutch the hat, make it safe, but he beat me to it.

'I've lost my job,' he said. 'I've worked hard, you know. It's just that it's last on, first off. It's not fair. I work bloody hard. Excuse the language, Miss, but I do. Not like the lazy Fred! The so-and-so. He's not lost his job.'

Anger bubbled. I agreed "lazy Fred" shouldn't have a job.

'We have a nice home and were going along so well. Now this. I can't bear to face her. I've let her down... again.'

I struggled to be positive. 'Look,' I said, 'the place where I work is understaffed. Maybe you could try them.'

'Where's that?' He sat a little straighter.

'Albury and Sons. Electrical fitters. They're on Leonora Street, off Brick Road.'

Desolate once again, his words were a new pain. 'I tried them last week. Mr Murray said they were putting off blokes. Not much work coming in.'

'Oh! I didn't know that.' I sucked in a quick breath. 'Hope my job is safe.'

'Yes, me too, Miss.' He forced a smile and stood. 'I'll go now. Trains coming. Thanks for trying. Will have to work something out. Our savings run out by the end of the month, and then I'll have to tell her about losing my job. I don't want to. I want her to be proud of me. Some husband I am. Not being able to support her and my kid. Hopeless bastard! Sorry, Miss. Goodbye.'

He scrunched the jacket under his arm and placed his hat back on while I was still trying to find words of wisdom. I watched him amble across the platform, his jacket dangling from his hand.

I knew I'd be in big trouble for being late, so I hurried towards the train heading in the other direction.

Bella and Candy repeatedly explained that it was quite reasonable for a good friend to at least have the decency to text them with an expected arrival time and not leave them pacing about on the city platform, looking like idiots.

I tried to explain the unusualness of my

encounter, but they were keen to start shopping.

Two dresses, one top, one pair of jeans and six glasses later, three friends sat around two milkshakes and a black tea.

'Well, that was awesome,' Candy said.

'I'll have something decent to drink out of now,' I said as I tore the corner from the parcel to peek at the patterned glasses.

Bella pushed her up-market paper bag onto the remaining space on the table, exposing the contents. 'Boring, you could have at least bought something to wear.'

'I needed the glasses. Lalita didn't like drinking juice from a mug.'

'You should have bought those trousers.'

Putting my purchase between my feet, I thought of the charcoal trousers I'd left on the rack and tugged at the belt I was wearing. 'Yeah, this would have gone well with them.'

'You could've bought a new belt.'

'Why?' I asked Candy. 'This one is perfectly okay.'

Candy spoke in single syllables, 'It's... not... new.'

'So what?'

She sighed and continued as if explaining to a child. 'It's out of that stupid box of bits, isn't it?'

I looked at the belt and pouted. 'Well, I like it, and I did end up with the aubergine top.'

'All I'm saying is you shouldn't be wearing something so old. You don't know who owned it.'

I thought of possibilities, convinced myself otherwise and finally steered the conversation around to my meeting with the strange fellow at the train station. 'I've seen him three times now, and he's always wearing that odd hat.'

'Did you find out his name?'

'No, but he said his wife lived in Redhill Road.'

Bella motioned to the waiter. 'Maybe you'll run into him there. Is it near your place?'

'Didn't ask; he was too busy talking about losing his job. That's another thing. He said he tried Albury's and they were laying people off.' I tried to think if I had heard any rumours about cutbacks.

Candy and Bella both stopped eating. Candy spoke first, 'You aren't going to lose your job, are you?'

'Don't know. Didn't think so until today. My boss just placed an ad in the paper for two new electricians last week. I emailed the stuff myself.'

'What else did the man in the hat say?'

I remembered his deep-set eyes hiding behind lowered eyebrows. I thought of the hat wobbling precariously on his leg. 'He talked about a Mr Murray, but I don't know anyone by that name. Might be the new manager over in the workshop, I suppose.'

'Better ask about it on Monday.'

'I will. Don't need to lose my job, now I've got rent to pay.'

It was dark when I reached Redhill Road, and I scurried into the building. I jumped at the figure stepping out of a shadowy corner.

'Mr Nelli! What are you doing hiding?'

'Sorry, Miss. I wasn't hiding, just awaiting for you. Didn't want to miss you.'

'What's up? I dropped the rent into your wife this morning.'

His elongated earlobes trembled as he shook his head. 'No, no, not the money. It is all very well. You up-to-date.' His teeth did their usual dance. 'I found newspaper clipping. You might like it.'

'Newspaper?' I stopped wishing he would let me pass without having to chat politely. 'About what?'

'Young couple once to live here. You see.'

My pulse raced. I put my shopping and

handbag down and accepted the faded page. All the implications I'd been trying to avoid danced over each other. Prams, hats, belts, and yelling fathers tumbled and twisted my psyche. The heading said: "Couple still missing". There were no pictures, and I decided it was better to take it and read it later.

'Looks... interesting. Can I take it with me?'

'You keep it. I don't want. It is too old.'

I tucked the page into my bag and picked up the new glasses with little care. After climbing the stairs with more haste than usual, I dumped my possessions on the kitchen bench, spread the newspaper and started reading.

"A young couple has been missing from their home in Redhill Road for a month. Mr Agnew, the father of Jocelyn, said he had searched everywhere for them. According to Mr Agnew, Oscar Stringer had been acting strangely since he went to the city for work. He hasn't returned home for his regular visit. Jocelyn Stringer and her small child were last seen in the local park. Fears are held for their safety."

I paced around the room, sucking in air,

flapping the newspaper against my thigh, furiously trying to clear my mind of demanding images. 'I won't believe it. Must be a coincidence. I will not let it be real.'

Thinking of Lalita's suggestion that these odd persons, who no one else saw, wanted to talk to me made me shiver despite my flushing face. I stood still for several minutes with my eyes closed, remembering all the times I refused to admit anything was unusual, trying to recall the encounters I'd had with the people who now seemed to be Jocelyn, Oscar and Mr Agnew... and then there was baby Kenny.

I screwed the article into a furious ball, tossed it at the rubbish bin and glared at it as it lay there without a worry in the world next to a banana skin.

Stomping around the kitchen, flinging dirty dishes into a sink of pre-used water, I used every swear word I could think of.

When that didn't stop the torment, I flung off my clothes, stood under a lukewarm shower, and cried.

After a sleepless night, a morning full of apprehension and an afternoon of numbness, I needed desperately to talk to one of my friends. Having seen enough of the odd rituals Lalita performed, even being part of them from time to time, my friends would at least be sympathetic.

They even thought it was fun to have a mother who let you call her by her first name—an invented one at that. I wasn't sure how either of them could help, but I needed their comforting presence.

Candy's phone went to voicemail, but I reached Bella and hastily issued myself an invitation to her place.

A train always seemed to take forever when one is in a hurry, and being on edge, I walked in circles, begging the train to arrive instantly.

A man rushed past, so close the air of his hurry almost took my scarf with it. I clutched my bag closer and swivelled my head. I wasn't surprised, certainly not shocked, to realise it was the young man in the fedora again. I called out to him; he turned and looked into my eyes, then moved on.

'Hey, Oscar. Stop,' I yelled.

He hesitated for a moment, then ran across the platform. An express train rushed through the station, and Oscar seemed to throw himself in front of it. My mind and body staggered. I grabbed hold of the back of a bench and gasped for air.

'You alright?' asked an unfamiliar face.

'What happened to him?' I begged.

'Who?'

'Oscar.' I plopped onto the bench and sagged over my knees. 'The man in the hat. He jumped in front of the train.'

The stranger shook his head. 'I think you're imagining it. Here, have some water.'

I sat straighter. 'He did. I saw him.'

'No, there wasn't anyone.'

Assisted by the stranger and scrutinised by several other commuters, I clambered up and went to the platform's edge. There was no sign of anyone having been hit by a train. There would have been bedlam if it had happened. I was the only one causing a stir.

'I was sure he jumped. Maybe he just disappeared behind someone. I feel a bit stupid.'

'No harm done.' The stranger retrieved his water bottle from me. 'Are you sure you're okay?'

Assuring the small gathering I could carry on without assistance, I placed my hand on the bulky buckle of my belt and wondered, why does it have to be me?

I rang Bella and told her I wasn't feeling well and would rather go home. She expressed her concern and offered to come over, but without giving much detail, I said I needed to sleep and would ring her the next day and explain.

Sleep didn't happen. I wrestled with the events of the last few weeks. I tried to believe it was my contorted imagination, but a forming awareness said otherwise. Things needed to be done. I'd have to solve this riddle—no one else. After creating a plan, I finally slept lightly until early morning.

Mrs Nelli responded quickly to my tapping on their door. I needed more information, and I prayed my landlord could help.

'I was hoping your husband might have some more newspaper cuttings. I'd like to find out more about the couple who lived upstairs.'

'He not here,' she said.

With an internal sigh of impatience, I said, 'It's okay, I can come back.'

'No, it's alright, Miss Asha, I help.' As she waddled away from the door, she added, 'He gathers many, many things. Too many, I say. But does he listen? No, he never listens.' She turned back to me, shrugged, and said, 'Perhaps he has more newspaper pieces. You please to wait. I look for you.'

After I'd stood in the hallway, stepping from one foot to the other, impatiently watching the minute hand reach five, Mrs Nelli widened the door again and handed me a box of papers.

'You can have, to look only. Then you return

them. He too busy today, but he won't mind you to look. But you return, please.'

I shoved my keys in my pocket and took the box. 'Thanks. I'll get them back to you as soon as possible.'

'Not to hurry.' She realigned her apron. 'I tell my husband you return them.'

I wondered where Mr Nelli and his energetic teeth were, but it was none of my business.

By the time I returned to my flat, Bella had arrived. She questioned me about my health. I assured her I'd recovered and filled her in as much as possible, which left her amazed and worried again.

'Who is this guy who keeps appearing? Why haven't you seen him before now?' She shifted in her seat. 'What does he want?'

Brushing the dust off my hands, I swivelled around and faced Bella. 'Isabella Elizabeth Grey, if I knew the answers to those questions, we wouldn't be rummaging through all this stuff. Just start searching.'

She picked up a magazine and turned it over. 'So, what are we looking for?'

'Don't know, really. But I guess anything that might have something to do with Oscar. Then there's the lady at the bus stop near the park. She'll be Josie. Oh, and the baby, Kenny.'

'It isn't easy looking for something when you don't know what you are looking for.'

'I know, but just keep reading. Mr Nelli kept one piece. Maybe he kept other local news items. I have a feeling they lived in this building. Perhaps even in this flat.'

'That's weird,' Bella said.

My shoulders drooped, and I turned over two pages without reading a word.

Rapid knocking on the door revealed an out-of-breath Candy. Keen not to miss anything, she'd run all the way from the bus stop.

'What have I missed? Fill me in.'

I caught her up with events. She retrieved the crumpled newspaper article from my waste bin and smoothed it out the best she could.

'Why don't you ring Lalita?' Candy asked.

'NO!' I screamed, scaring my friends. 'Sorry.' I grinned with the apology. 'I don't want to tell her more than she already knows. She'd be here demanding all sorts of explanations, and I don't have any yet. You mustn't tell her.'

'Okay,' shrugged Candy.

Bella shook the dust from a crumbling page. 'Sure, it's just between you and us.'

'Promise.'

'Yep,' Bella said.

Candy formed an imaginary zip across her lips. 'Mmm...'

Reading old newspapers can be quite interesting but equally, excessively boring.

'Didn't know he was married to her.'

'Why would Mr Nelli keep that?'

'Turn it over, stupid.'

'Oh, yes. Another piece about Italy.'

We stopped for a sandwich and changed the topic of conversation to boyfriends, outfits and jobs.

'Did you ask your boss about your job, Asha?'

'Yep. That's another odd thing. He said the workshop manager is a Zac Matthews. Unless Oscar got the name wrong, it makes no sense at all. My boss reckons we have several places available.'

'Weird.'

'Don't say that.'

'What?'

'Weird.'

'Why?'

'I don't want to be weird.' I let a cutting fall from my hand, stood and walked to the window. 'Everyone talks about Lalita being weird. I don't want everyone saying that about me.'

'Asha, it's okay.' Candy came up behind me and placed her hand on my arm. 'Lalita may be a little odd, but she's lovely. Nothing wrong with being a bit weird.'

'Not me, I want to be normal.'

Candy giggled and poked me in the ribs. 'What's normal?'

I was about to clarify people who didn't see auras and talk to dead people, when Bella yelled, 'Hey! Look, this might be something.'

'What?' Candy and I scampered over to Bella.

Bella waved a scrappy piece of paper at me. 'It's a birth announcement. "Oscar and Jocelyn announce the birth of Kenneth William".'

A clammy feeling ran up my back and I had to sit down. 'Oh!'

Candy sat down next to me and stared into my face. 'What now?'

The heat reached my face. I bunched my fingers into a ball and tried to stay calm. 'It's them. All of them. The hat man. The bus stop lady, her baby was Kenny. Wasn't sure before, but I bet the other man who came in here yelling for Josie was her father.'

'What man?'

'Didn't I tell you about the crazy man who raced around this room demanding I find Josie?'

Both girls spoke an emphatic 'no' before

Candy asked, 'What about the baby. Kenny. When did you see him?'

Throwing a magazine onto the pile of discarded papers, I stood and turned away from them. I breathed deeply and waited a few moments before speaking. 'I didn't really see Kenny. I spoke to his mother at the bus stop near the park. She's obviously Jocelyn.'

'Hey, this is great.'

'No, it isn't.'

We didn't find anything else and several hours later, my friends left me alone with my crazy thoughts.

It was dusk as I left my flat. I needed space to think. Wandering along the streets, past the park where I had seen Jocelyn and baby Kenny, I found myself drawn to the river.

I remembered Josie recounting Oscar and her walks along a stretch of sand. She'd said it was a special place, a time of love for them. I hoped to find them there.

After leaving the footpath, I went down the steps to the grass and lingered before heading towards the riverbank.

Pacing purposely across the firm sand, I called their names repeatedly and hoped they would answer. Perhaps I could find a sign, discover how I could help, but when I heard nothing except my voice, I asked my grandmother to intervene and bring it all to a happy ending.

The soft glow of the last rays of sunlight shone across the water presenting a picturesque scene. Mellowed by the view and a little less frightened by the forces of possibilities, I sat on some rocks and fingered the little toy truck I'd casually picked up from my ever-wobbly coffee table. I assumed it belonged to Kenny at some time.

I unwound the striped scarf and let the gentle breeze cool me. I had walked determinedly, trying to out-stride the realisation, but now I let all the emotions of the past weeks wash over me. Could Lalita be right? Was there a way for the departed to contact the living? I had moments of clarity throughout my life, but the prospects of dealing with it frightened me. Lalita wanted it to be true, but she studied and practised to no avail, while I refused all attempts, desperately wanting it not to be possible.

I spun the wheels of the little truck and let them wind to a halt. The sun was all but gone when I saw the pram. An unwavering young woman pushed it through the sand. She swore with the effort and yelled at the child to stay still. I jumped to my feet and ran towards her.

'Jocelyn, wait up. Please, Josie, wait,' I called as I ran across the wet sand. She turned and seemed to hear me but pushed on. Now the wheels sank into the sloppy sand, and any forward motion became impossible.

I called again as I drew closer, then I tripped. 'Shit! Josie, wait.'

Cursing continuously, I squeezed river water from my shirt and stomped sand from my jeans.

Due to the fading light, retrieving the contents of my handbag took some time. I didn't find the tiny toy. Jocelyn and Kenny were gone. Just like the first time I saw them, they had disappeared in an instant.

I'd hoped the river would give me answers, but it only provided more riddles. I wound the scarf tightly around my neck and headed for home. Striding out against the breeze, I didn't see him until he spoke.

'Excuse me. Have you seen a lady with a pram?'

I stopped, looked up, squinted at him as he came down the steps. 'I did, but they've gone again.'

'Where did they go?' The elderly man's eyes flicked from right to left. 'I must find them.'

I tried to catch his eye, but he kept glancing past me, down to the river's edge.

'They disappeared,' I said. 'Very quickly. Perhaps you can explain how it happens?'

Finally, he looked directly at me. 'You saw them. Please, which way did they go?'

I pointed to where I'd seen them. 'They were down by the water; the pram got stuck in the sand. Then I tripped. Sorry, but I didn't see her after that.'

'I have to find them.' He stepped sideways. 'She must come home.' He moved further away from me. 'It's all so sad.'

I wanted to ask a thousand more questions, but he refused to stop. Following him as he hurried across the grass to the sand, I kept up as best I could. I was shivering from the dampness and although I didn't like to admit it, from the emotional strain as well.

Once at the river's edge, we walked up and down in the dark. He stumbled. I almost grabbed him, but he recovered quickly and pressed on with me alongside.

As the half-moon peeked out from behind slow-moving clouds, I stared at him, memorising every whisker, every wrinkle on his life-worn face. Is he of this world?

We continued to search for signs of life as we squelched along the bank, dodging the waves washing away all trace of the pram's furrows.

'You're the man who came to my flat. You're Jocelyn's father, aren't you?' I asked.

The man swung around. 'You know my Josie?'

'Not really.' I stopped, caught my breath as he paced back to me. 'I met her at the bus stop once.'

'When?' he demanded.

'A week or two back. She was walking Kenny in the pram.'

His breath reached my forehead as he asked, 'Did she say anything about Oscar losing his job?'

'Well, she told me he'd lost one job and moved to the city. She was concerned because he hadn't come home when she expected him.'

'I have to find her.' His eyes moistened. 'She'll be devastated when she finds out about Oscar.'

'What happened to Oscar?' I asked, hoping I didn't already know the answer.

Mr Agnew looked like he had the weight of the world on his shoulders as he sank onto one of the rocks, ignoring his water-soaked shoes. I'd had my fill of wet sand for one day, and as we had been walking for quite some time, had almost dried out with the generated heat.

I removed my coat and scarf and placed them

on the rocks. I walked down to the water's edge and looked across the river, noticing the rising fog. Admitting my world was becoming weirder by the day, I retraced my steps to the rocks, ready to confront anything he might tell me.

I hadn't counted on Mr Agnew leaving.

I swiped at my belongings, removing them from the rocks and flinging them over my shoulder, yelping sharply as a button hit my cheek.

Twelve

I knew I had to; I just didn't want to.

Bella and Candy would listen again, but—?

No, I would have to tell Lalita.

Two sleepless nights later, I presented a frightful sight to my mother when I stood on her doorstep in dirty clothes. After trying to interrupt the streams of instructions on how I should be looking after myself better, and numerous offers of remedies for the stricken soul, I gave in and let her have her say. When she stopped issuing her special kind of advice and finally listened, Lalita flitted between excitement and worry as I drifted through the story.

'How do you do it?' was one excited question.

'I have no idea.'

'What has it to do with you?' asked my worried mother.

'I have no idea.'

She spent an anxious time delving through her extensive book collection in the hope of finding something to guide us.

Discarded books built a pile on the floor while she turned several page corners down for future reference. Meanwhile, I sat mesmerised by nothing and everything. Crouched down on the floor sipping camomile tea, hoping to restore my symmetry, I longed to be five again and able to make it all go away by scrunching up my eyes and chanting, 'Go away, go away.'

'We must find out what they want from you,' Lalita decided.

'Can't we just make them go away?'

'Obviously not.'

'Damn.'

She chanted, resplendent in the purple gown she'd hastily donned for full effect. I sat obligingly on the mediation cushion, sullen and disinterested. I dozed from time to time, glad of the respite from thinking. Still Lalita chanted. And three hours later as agitation set in, she blamed me for not trying harder.

'I never try at all. They just appear, and then they disappear just as quickly.'

'You could at least try something. Chant with me.'

'No, Lalita. I think I'll go home.'

'Please stay. We'll eat and try again.'

'No, I really have to go. I'm worn out. I have to go to work on Monday.'

'I thought you had leave.'

'Just this week.'

'Well, you must stay tonight... and Sunday. It is time for me to tell you the full story about your gift.'

'I don't want to have "The Gift", as you put it, and I don't need you to rant on about it. Now is not the time. I have to figure it all out myself.'

'Asha, dear. I haven't told you before, but your grandmother had The Gift.'

'The Gift! What? All the stuff you keep insisting we do. Is that what you mean?'

'Sort of.'

My whole body sagged as I sat. 'Well, I knew she did stuff... with cards. I sort of remember her chanting... and her incense. Candles... yeah. I knew you thought she was special, but—' I shrugged, 'I thought you were just... being you.'

She touched my shoulder and smiled. 'Thanks, I think. However, it was a little more than that. Throughout my childhood, she would often drift into a trance-like state and speak to spirits. It never frightened me; it seemed so natural. Father huffed and puffed about it and would disappear to the pub whenever she had meetings with like-minded people. I would sneak out of my bed and listen to them.'

This revelation amazed me, and I sat with my

hands over my mouth as she kept talking.

'I read all her books and copied her little rituals, determined to follow her ways. Your Grandma Rosie looked like any other woman on the street, but oh, how different she was when she spoke. Her soft, gentle voice could have calmed a street full of noisy protesters in no time at all.

'Rosie drew people to her, and she loved everyone. My father tolerated it. That's about all I could say really to describe his reactions. It was often the case where he would come home to find the Tarot cards across the kitchen table or an unknown person sobbing in Rosie's embrace. He would impart a gruff greeting and head towards his shed. Goodness knows what he did in there. It was out of bounds to us mere females.

'He used to tease Rosie about her ability. My mother would ask him what he had been doing in the shed, and he would reply, "Surely you know! Doesn't your all-seeing third eye penetrate a mere tin shed?" She would reply with words like, "You'd better not be doing anything you shouldn't; otherwise, the dead will visit the shed and turn it upside down." It was just banter between two oddly matched people who loved each other deeply.'

I interrupted, 'Didn't Grandfather mind all the candles and garbage around the place?'

Lalita stood and paced around the room before replying. 'Oh, Asha. Do you really think it's garbage?' She dropped down next to me and took my hand. 'I'm so sorry, honey. I really am a silly woman.'

I realised I'd been a little harsh and stroked her forearm. Before I could say anything, she continued.

'I idolised my mother and wanted to be like her. I wanted the affection of the masses as she had. We would walk down the street, and everyone knew Rosie Underwood. They would smile or nod their greeting. I wanted to be like her.

'When I was a teenager, I started wearing gypsy-style clothes, placing candles and objects of the occult around my room, trying desperately to seek contact with the spirits. Rosie would shake her head and tell me all the trimmings didn't matter; The Gift would take care of itself. However, she let me decorate my room as I wanted, even though it contrasted with their down-to-earth, comfortable furniture and minimal decorations. She had one small dresser in the dining room with some candles and oddments of faith, but that was all. Outwardly, my mother and our home were like anyone else's. Father died when I was sixteen, so it was just the two of us. I became obsessed with learning all I could. I thought by gaining knowledge, I would gain the ability I craved.'

Lalita sat motionless with her hands in her lap. She stared across the room, not seeing anything. 'I really am a charlatan. I knew long ago I hadn't been blessed with insight into the spirit world. However, I watched Rosie and hoped something would change. It was after you were born my longed-for change came.'

She moved the cushions from behind her and expelled a long breath through her mouth. I thought this might be my chance to find out about my father and offered to make us some tea. As I brought the pot and cups back into the lounge room, I bravely asked, 'How did you meet my father? Was he gifted?'

She poured the tea, and one could almost hear the steam wafting from the cups, as if a great vacuum surrounded my question.

After picking up a cup, blowing across the liquid and sipping slowly, she finally spoke, 'Well, we needn't go there. It isn't important to what I am trying to tell you at the moment.' Lalita shook her head, but I could see her eyes take on some long-forgotten pain.

'Lalita, we do need to talk about it. Shouldn't I know about my father?'

Her mouth drooped, and she moved away from me to sit hunched in the single chair opposite. I waited patiently for a reply.

'Maybe another time,' came her whisper.

I glared at her, hoping to make her understand my need. 'I've asked so many times. It's time you stopped being so vague. He's my father, for goodness' sake. I need more than a birth date and waffling half-stories.'

She flung herself out of the chair and stalked down the passage to her room. Her hasty movement panicked me, and I wanted to rush after her, but I sat, drained, waiting, hoping this time I might get some answers. Several minutes later, she returned, sat by my side and placed a chocolate box on my lap.

'This is all I have of him,' she said, and the pain in her eyes intensified.

The box contained a few photos, a man's watch, a twig of rosemary and a matchbox. I stared at each faded shot of young people obviously in love: one in a park, one at an ocean, several of a hippie-style wedding. I recognised my mother and became transfixed by the revelation of my father. He was tall and fragile-looking with long hair and a moustache. I grinned back at his radiant smile directed at his new wife—ecstatic that at last, I knew for sure I had been born of love.

After learning as much as these photos offered, I turned to the other items. I held the watch, closed my eyes, and tried to feel my father's soul. A warm glow covered me, and the tears running down my cheeks didn't embarrass me. A touch of a hand on my shoulder told me my mother cared, and my gentle tears turned to a torrent accompanied by violent sobbing.

'Why didn't you give me this before?' I demanded after regaining control. 'What good has it done for me not to see these?'

Lalita gripped her hands together, looked away from my face and spoke in between sniffs and gasps of sad memories. 'Too painful. I loved him, you know. I drove him away. He couldn't stand my desire to be like my mother. He said I should grow up. Stop wishing for something I didn't have.' She swallowed deliberately and wiped her hand across her top lip. 'He was right, you know. I just never realised it soon enough.'

She paused again and fingered the piece of rosemary that dropped its leaves as she removed it from the box. Carefully picking up each speck of a leaf, she finally looked me in the eyes. 'He died. I couldn't stand it. He died before I could see sense. It was too hard to talk about. When he left, I focused on giving you a happy home. If I talked about your father, Robert, if I talked about him, it would emphasise he wasn't here, so I refused. Oh, dear Robbie. I still miss him, so, so terribly much.'

As the intense emotion of her memories flooded my brain, I tried to deflect any more distress.

'How young? Where did he go? I asked and then hesitated. 'Sorry, maybe we shouldn't talk about it right now.'

Lalita's slow smile released some of the terrible pain giving her a haunted look. She rose from the couch and signalled me into her arms. We stood wrapped with emotions until she spoke, 'I will tell you more.' She gently pushed me away to arm's length, still holding my hand. 'Yes, I'll explain about your father and why our house is draped in colours of the rainbow with every candle colour known to man and incense sticks peeking out of every drawer. The two stories overlap a great deal. I owe you an explanation, and if you can bear with me, it will be today.'

I wrapped a worn mohair rug around my body and waited. Lalita, meanwhile, had disappeared into the kitchen and turned on the kettle. She returned sometime later, having changed from the outrageous purple dress into what was for her, a more sedate outfit of calico trousers and a blue hand-knitted jumper, bringing with her some herbal tea. We sipped the hot drink between darting glances at each other. My need to know more about my background was tempered with the feeling of what our own Pandora's Box might reveal. I remembered the quotation; *be careful what you wish for*, and uneasiness crept into my mind. Once the level of hot liquid reached halfway, Lalita settled into the cosiness of the chair and began her story.

'Robbie and I went to live with your grandmother after we were married. It was a big house, and we had little money. Rosie didn't like being on her own, so it was practical for all of us. It was a good arrangement. You were born twelve months later, and I thought I had a perfect life. Your father suffered from asthma and found it difficult to hold down regular work. He wasn't often out of work for long but moved between jobs quite regularly. He wouldn't give up his cigarettes and blamed everything else for his cough. Rosie used to be on at him all the time to stop. She'd tell him how badly it affected his aura and continually offered concoctions with the intention of doing him some good. I nagged him to listen to my mother. "Rosie knows what she's talking about," I would say. He tired of two "insane" women bleating about his one and only vice. One day, he just upped and left. No warning, well, not in so many words. He packed a small suitcase and left. I didn't hear from him for about six months, and then it was a letter from the other side of the country saying he had found a good job and would send some money when he could. I was hoping he would miss us and come back, but he died about four months later. His sister sent me his belongings—next to nothing. A case of clothes and the chocolate box was it.'

Lalita came and sat close to me and pulled the corner of the rug over her knees. There was a quietness about her I had never experienced, and I loathed to break the mood.

'I loved him,' she whispered. 'I was devastated when he left. If I hadn't had you... I don't know if I could have carried on. Your grandmother was a great strength, and she insisted the cards had only good things for us. The three of us drifted along through the regular variety of life, highlighted by the blessings that seemed to come Rosie's way. You were a good baby, having funny conversations with yourself and constantly smiling. When Rosie declared it was because a special guardian angel watched over you, I was thrilled. I knew my mother could comprehend things other people didn't, and as any mother will tell you, they just want the very best for their child. Apparently, all your goo-ing and gaa-ing wasn't any ordinary baby noises; it was direct contact with the angels. The smiles were your way of being pleased with their presence.'

'No kidding!' I exclaimed.' You mean I was weird right from the start?'

'Asha-lee! It's not weird to be blessed with the gift of seeing beyond the everyday.'

'Certainly feels weird to me.' I wriggled into a more comfortable spot. 'Being visited by people who are supposed to be dead; if that's not weird, I don't know what is!'

'Do you want to hear more or not?'

'Of course I do. It's just that I've spent years thinking you were making it all up. I just wanted it all to go away. I hated those terrible girls at school laughing at me. I didn't want to be sniggered at as I walked up the street. It was awful. I wanted just to be like everyone else. I never saw the benefit of the so-called Gift.'

'I do understand, honey, but you said yourself, you can't help it. The Gift is there whether you want it or not. Do you know, from when you were two, you had imaginary friends?'

My sarcastic chuckle didn't amuse her.

'I know, I know. So do lots of children. There really is little proof, but with your grandmother's knowledge, we were sure yours were children who had passed over. One was called Beth. Do you remember her?'

'You've got to be kidding!' I pulled the rug up to my chin.

'Well, I do,' Lalita said. 'She was a naughty child and would tip things over all the time. Rosie had to have a real stern talk with her to get her to stop. Then there was Jimmy, but he didn't hang around long after he found there were no males in the house. Rosie tried to explain to him it didn't matter, but he took all your dresses off the hangers, and we found them in the bath.'

'Shit! You're making that up,' I said.

'No. And—

'I know, I know.' I could have used much more colourful language. 'Really?'

'Yes. It's true. Then when you were nearly four, you asked if Jessica could join us for dinner. I struggled. Thank goodness for Rosie calming things down. You see, it was so hard for me, what with you and your grandmother often chatting away to an uncle who died sixteen years previously. I felt left out and would sit in wonderment, not really knowing whether both of you were pulling my leg or not.'

She ignored my interruption of amazement and continued, 'Then Rosie died. Dear, sweet Rosie. How sad you were. We both were. The pain she went through with the cancer was horrid. You refused to go to the funeral proclaiming Rosie would be back soon and you didn't want to see her in a big black box. After the funeral, you would sit in Rosie's bed and talk in a singing kind of way I could only assume was your way of talking to her.'

Lalita rubbed her hands together, bringing the blood to the surface in an attempt to warm them.

A memory flash of Rosie's laughter made me smile. 'I remember that day,' I said.

Lalita nodded slowly and continued her story, 'I was determined to let you develop your gift. That was why I had to learn as much as I could. That was why I did all those crazy things. I was trying to educate you in Rosie's absence. She had eagerly anticipated the opportunity to pass on her knowledge but didn't want to overwhelm you as a small child, so she waited. Then it was too late. I tried to fill the void. Without her to show you weren't the only one with The Gift, you became scared and refused to learn. That day your grandmother spoke to you, I was exhilarated. Finally, Rosie would let you know it was all going to be okay. But you turned away from her.'

I sat with my chin resting on my bent knees. I didn't know what to say. Was there anything to be said? I doubted it.

Silence hung between us as we both absorbed our private thoughts. I realised she expected me to tell her everything was alright. This was the part in the story where mother and daughter hugged and expressed their understanding of everything gone before. However, I hesitated.

She thought she had been doing the right thing—so? Shouldn't I have had a say in the matter? Perhaps not when I was a toddler, but really, one could expect to be able to handle the responsibility once one reached a certain age.

I looked up from under my eyelashes with a scowl across my face. I was shocked to see my mother wiping away tears from her dejected countenance. It hit me like a tornado would a glasshouse. My skin prickled, and my heart jumped. Here was my ever-radiant mother looking like the proverbial death warmed up.

'I'm sorry. Really, I am,' I said. 'I've been so hard on you. I thought you wanted to be in the spotlight with everyone putting you on a pedestal because you gave them something they couldn't get elsewhere. It wasn't that, was it? I can see now; it was all about the love you had for your mum. That was why you tried so hard to have me do this stuff, wasn't it?'

She turned her face to mine, and I could see a smile forming.

'That... yes... that was part of it. It was also about you. Rosie was so comfortable in what she did. It brought her pleasure. I only wanted you to feel the same.'

I reached and took her hand, relieved the moment of tension had passed. 'I love you. You're certainly different from everyone else's mum, but you're mine and I love you.'

'Thanks, sweetheart. Now you know about Rosie and your father, I feel much better, but I have one more thing for you.'

'Oh no, not more revelations.' I frowned and shook my head but then softened my anxiousness with a smile.

'This one is a nice one,' she said, and she reached for the chocolate box which held my father's mementos, placing it on the couch beside us. She handed me the matchbox we had previously overlooked.

'Here, this is for you. Your father sent it to me for you. It was another thing I couldn't deal with.'

I opened the battered matchbox and tipped the contents onto my other hand. There lay a tangled gold chain with a beautiful single pearl attached. I was dumbfounded.

'It's gorgeous. How? When?' I started.

'He sent it for your birthday. Years ago, of course. You were too young for it at the time, so I put it away. I honestly forgot it was there. When I did remember, I couldn't bear the idea of you wearing it and reminding me of my loss. Rather selfish.'

I hugged her and thanked her for the story and the belated gift. 'I probably wouldn't have appreciated it before now. I truly think it's a part of my growing.'

We talked for many hours before we were both exhausted and, without eating, we fell into our beds.

Thirteen

It was so nice to wake up in my old bed, and I snuggled down again for a few pleasant minutes. I had unconsciously tossed and turned in the early part of the night, fighting against the recurring dream, but the dream prevailed, and I clearly remember the different ending. The fan shape twisted above my head as it always had, but instead of dropping tears, it landed at my feet and clear water rushed over it. I stood and watched it wallow in the calm waters before a bird came and grabbed it. The fan opened and revealed a beautiful string of pearls that fell over my head. All but one pearl disappeared into the soft sand, and I stood with the last one in my hand. Wonderful music played... and then I woke, contented with the knowledge something had changed.

Sometime later, I padded into the kitchen, ravenously looking for something to eat. After some toast and hummus and armed with a hot drink, I informed Lalita it was my turn to tell a story. She listened intently as I repeated my dream with its happy ending.

'Your father is talking to you.'

'Why do you say that? You said he didn't have the gift.'

'The pearl. It was hidden all those years. Now you have it. It was him telling you he is pleased about it.'

'No, but I do think it has something to do with him. I think maybe now I have his pearl, the dream is no longer necessary.'

'Yes, yes, of course.' Lalita rose quickly and celebrated with arms flailing and legs moving in something resembling a dance.

'Lalita, you're insane.' I laughed.

With a final twirl, she asked, 'Aren't you happy too?'

'Time will tell if the dream comes back, but yes, I'm happy. The pearl is beautiful, and I'm pleased you've given it to me. Now just to solve the other dead people's problem.'

'Asha!'

'What now?'

'Surely you can be a little more sensitive.'

My eyebrows rose. 'Oh. Okay.' I lowered my voice and imitated an American gangster archetype, 'Do you want to hear about the visitations... or not?'

'Of course, of course.'

'First, I need coffee. And not your pretend stuff. This... yep, I need coffee.'

Finding some in the back of her pantry and with goat's milk added, we snuggled under the mohair rug, Lalita grimacing with every sip of the unfamiliar.

'I am sure there is something I have to do to help them leave this realm together,' I said. 'It's so new to me, and it's puzzling. It seems that when I wear the belt, Oscar appears. I gather the wooden truck is the means by which Josie appeared the first time. Remember, I was coming to visit you and the lady with the pram told me all about her troubles. That was Josie. What do you think I should do? How can I solve the riddle for them?'

'It seems it all has to do with the items you found, so I guess you have to do something with them.' Lalita decided the coffee was far too awful and refused to finish it, while I swallowed the last few mouthfuls purposefully.

After going over the incidents several times without resolution, Lalita offered, 'Why don't you meditate and see what's revealed to you?'

I protested half-heartedly. Lalita pulled the rug away, roughly folded it and tossed it into the other chair.

'Look,' she repeated, 'Meditation might work. After all, they got in touch with you, not the other way around. Perhaps they will again.'

With no better option, I returned home and spent the afternoon doing as Lalita suggested. I sat in the middle of my bed and tried to clear my mind, asking for guidance.

For two weeks, I spent each evening after work in the same position. Bella and Candy kept texting and ringing me, demanding to know what was going on and why I wasn't responding. All I could offer was I was busy trying to resolve this seemingly unresolvable dilemma and asked them to be patient. Lalita was easier to waylay after knowing meditation was involved and only rang once a day. With nothing coming from the outer reaches of the psychic realm, I was just beginning to believe I had seen the last of Mr Agnew and his family when Mr Nelli brought them to my attention again.

'Miss, Miss,' he called as I came through the front doorway. 'You see this. I found it last night. You may like it.'

His teeth talked even when he had stopped. I found it hard not to stare.

He gave me another newspaper article, and although my impulse was to snatch and run, I remembered my manners before retreating.

"The mystery of Jocelyn Stringer's disappearance continues to baffle the police. Mr Oscar Stringer fell to his death at the Redhill Station last week, although some doubt has been raised about whether it may have been suicide. Mr Stringer lost his job from the local brick manufacturer, and his workmate, Mr Fred McNab, was quoted as saying, 'Oscar took it hard and was most disillusioned when he left on Friday. I wouldn't be surprised; he didn't know how to tell his wife.' However, inquiries reveal that the station was crowded, and the likelihood of him missing his footing while running for the train may have caused Mr Stringer's death."

I stared at the page, unable to believe what I was reading. I carefully unfolded the clipping and continued reading.

"There has been no trace of Mrs Stringer since the time of Mr Oscar Stringer's sacking, and Mr Agnew (Jocelyn Stringer's father) reports he has been unable to substantiate any of her movements for several weeks. The couple's young son, Kenneth James (aged six months), is also missing. Mr and Mrs Stringer were a

devoted couple, and the police fear the news of Oscar's death may have caused distress and disorientation to his wife. Anyone knowing the whereabouts of Mrs Jocelyn (Josie) Stringer and Kenneth should contact their local police immediately."

The photograph of Josie and Kenneth showed the young lady I had encountered at the bus stop all those weeks ago. The story revealed to me grew clearer, but there were many unanswered questions. The unfathomable ones: why? And, why me?

Then, if I could ever find an answer to those two, what was I supposed to do about it? No amount of meditating had brought answers, so now what?

I shifted the esky and all the other storage items from the bottom of the kitchen pantry and opened the box that had yielded all the drama. I spread each item out on my couch, along with the belt and scarf from my wardrobe. The wooden truck lay somewhere on the riverbank. I sat on the floor staring at each one in turn. Were they just leftover junk, or were they the necessary pieces for resolution as Lalita suggested? Where do I go from here?

When no answer came, I plonked the items back in the box and turned on the telly.

It was Wednesday before I decided recovering the toy should be my first course of action.

Arriving at the river, I strolled across the sand and started searching. The tide could have taken the toy into its depth, or someone else might have claimed it. With this thought, I became anxious, as finding it suddenly seemed imperative. I removed my shoes and the icy water bit into my legs as I paddled past its edge. There were many small rock outcrops, and I searched fruitlessly for some time.

'Shit! Ouch!' I exclaimed as I caught my foot on something in the water.

Sitting down on a convenient rock, I studied my foot. No real damage. I rubbed it furiously, easing the pain. I returned to the water and recommenced my search. With waterlogged jeans and wet sleeves, I ignored my desire to head home, kicked at strands of seaweed and fiercely poked into crannies. Finally, I found the small toy bobbing in a rock pool. It was missing a wheel and the watery bath had distorted its body.

The river had been a special place for Oscar and Josie, and I hoped it would somehow be the catalyst for the final piece of the puzzle.

The following weekend, armed with a trowel, I took Oscar's belt and Kenny's toy down to the river on a bitterly cold night. The blustery wind shook my resolve, but the elements suited me, as I knew I would be less likely to run into any other living person.

I spent a few minutes digging by the rocks. The hole needed to be deep, and I laboured, building up perspiration even on the freezing winter's night. The water lapped into the hole, so I had to start again, this time further away from the river.

Satisfied with my excavating, I stood back and cradled Oscar and Kenny's belongings in my hands for a few moments. They had altered my life, but now they needed to finalise theirs. I dropped the items into the hole, patted them down with the blade of the trowel and headed home.

Each evening, I hurried home from work and walked to the river. I spent a couple of hours sitting, waiting and watching for something to happen.

My mind went over the events of the last few months. A simple box of possessions had turned my life upside down. I had spent years demanding to be normal, while always finding it hard to ignore the signs of my ability.

Was this why I was always so angry with Lalita? Did she realise the potential in the young child who refused to sit still on a meditation cushion while muttering about her dead grandmother's conversation? Had I refused to admit my psychic awareness because I didn't know how to control it? I could hardly refuse it anymore, could I?

Thursday night, I paced across the sands, willing something to happen. Friday night, I chanted soft words with hope. Nothing seemed to work, and I gradually became disillusioned.

Maybe humour would help. 'Oscar, Oscar, wherefore art thou, Oscar?'

Unfortunately, the universe didn't respond to my pathetic comedy, and it was yet another night I went home talking to myself.

On Saturday, I sat crossed-legged on my couch and concentrated. After twenty minutes of blankness, I realised my legs weren't used to being a pretzel and unfurled them, releasing the blood flow. I folded my arms and sighed repeatedly. Something had to move the spirits. Surely Josie and Oscar's story needed a successful conclusion, and for some reason, I was to be a part of it?

Dragging out the cardboard box that had started this confusion, I plucked out the remaining pieces from its depths. The jewellery box and the necklace held my attention, and I rolled the broken thread of pretty glass pieces into the palm of my hand. I ran my fingers over the beads. Had they been a gift from Oscar? I stared at the colours: bright red, sea green and a nondescript blue. I could imagine Josie being delighted and demanding they be clasped around her neck immediately. She would have paraded across the room, showing them off to an admiring husband. I bet she wore them often. They were bright enough to attract the attention of a toddler. Perhaps Kenny had broken them, pulling on them while held in his mother's arms. I wondered if any beads were lost.

With my mind elsewhere, I bumped the jewellery box and it fell to the floor. Reacting, my arm twitched, and I dropped the beads, gasping as I watched them scatter across the wooden floor in all directions.

'Exactly what I didn't need,' I yelled.

I scrambled after each bead, cursing the need to crawl around on my hands and knees. I dumped the collected beads into the box and told them to behave. I made myself some green tea before sitting, resolutely staring at the bead-filled box, demanding it reveal the next part of the story. Rosie kept entering my thoughts, and I wished she were here to guide me, but my grandmother refused to cooperate.

Fourteen

The moon was in its full splendour, an ideal glow for all matter of psychic phenomena to occur. My stomach behaved like an out-of-control blender even after spending the Saturday afternoon meditating, surrounded by the aromas of incense I had been taught would intensify cosmic connections. Anything was possible. I just hoped something would happen.

I wrapped what I now believed to be Mr Agnew's scarf tightly under my coat, added a ridiculous-looking beanie and stalked off to the river, blowing puffs of unsaid words.

Sitting on the rocks and remembering how Oscar and Josie had cared for each other, I knew they should be together.

They were young people, probably my age, struggling to come to terms with separation and disappointment. Life became unbearable for them. How sad they weren't strong enough to offer Kenny a good life.

I hoped I could be strong enough to face what life threw at me. It wasn't going to be easy. Being different never is.

The moon peeked out from behind a cloud and its silvery strands grasped down to the water's edge, reflecting its full beauty. I stood and admired nature's wonder.

Then it happened.

Oscar and Josie walked along the river's edge, hand in hand, leaning towards each other, totally absorbed by their love. Tucked on Oscar's hip and held tightly by his other hand, Kenny giggled as his parents spoke. Josie lifted her hand to caress her child's face. They were too far away for me to hear their words.

They wandered into the moonbeams and disappeared together.

It was inevitable I would cry. This was the end of a turbulent love story, a happy ending, nonetheless.

But were my tears for them or for me? Their story had concluded. But what about me? What events needed to pass in my life? Would mine be just as turbulent?

I thought of my grandmother and wondered if she hovered as Lalita had insisted a psychic grandmother would. I thought of my mother, who had revealed so many things to me. I kicked at the sand and stamped into the remains of a wave. A swift breeze sent a spray of sand and water across my face. I pulled my coat close and willed my legs to move again.

I could see someone standing at the top of the steps, and the outline looked familiar. After pacing across the grass, I climbed the steps to the footpath two at a time. I reached the top quickly and came face-to-face with Mr Agnew.

'Hello. On your way home?'

He came close enough for me to touch, but I hesitated. 'Hi, Mr Agnew. Yes.' I pointed to the water's edge. 'Did you see Josie and Oscar?'

A radiance covered his face, and his eyes shone. I imagined he wanted to dance. 'Yes, dear, I did.'

'I'm glad they're together.'

Nodding with quick, cheerful movements, he said, 'Yes, yes. And thank you for your help. Now I can go too.'

It was wrong to think of delaying him, but the moment seemed precious. I unravelled the scarf from my neck and held it out to him. 'Do you want your scarf?'

'No, you keep it. Keep it and be happy. Where I'm going, I won't need it.' He winked and chuckled at his departing humour. With a smile across his face, which had not been there during our other meetings, he walked down the steps, crossed to the sand, and faded like smoke on a windy day.

I stood for several minutes with the scarf in my extended hands, unable to move. My body trembled, my stomach complained, and my face couldn't decide if it should smile or succumb to the sadness. I thought about Oscar and Josie and the strength of love. The strangeness of the past weeks slipped away, and my soul tingled as joy replaced the melancholia.

Finally, I relaxed, and with the scarf trailing from my shoulder, I walked home.

Mr Nelli was dusting the banister when I walked in. I let the door bang and skipped up the steps. 'Lovely evening for it,' I said.

He eased into an upright position; stared as I twirled the scarf above my head.

'You be alright, Miss?' he asked.

I hesitated and gathered the scarf into a ball. 'You know what, Mr Nelli, I am. Yes, I think everything has turned out perfectly.'

The End

From the Author

My characters become friends as their story develops, visiting me at odd times, sharing their plans–but rarely bringing cake!

Asha first greeted me way back in August 2012. It's taken a while to create the correct aura of this interesting character and find the right publishing home for her. Thanks to Lisa and Rebekah at Dragonfly Publishing for their literary and literal welcome to Asha and me.

Without the ongoing support, knowledge and friendship of the members of Gosnells Writers Circle and Women's Writefree Writers Group, this story may still be on my hard drive. Many thanks to you all.

I couldn't continue this writing adventure without the valuable encouragement of my non-writing reader friends, who giggle and sigh in the right places as they talk about my books. Thank you.

And forever–love and hugs to my family.

I hope the readers of *The House on Redhill Corner* will be inspired to embrace their own unique qualities.

About the Author

Barbara Gurney's writing has been described as lyrical with a strong narrative. Often news items influence her poems while over-heard life experiences are hidden in longer works.

She says, 'I'm fascinated by the impact history has on people's lives – both of country and of family. I also believe there are some spiritual, or supernatural, aspects of the world which are constantly in the background, waiting to affect our lives.'

She joined Gosnells Writers Circle in 2008 and Writefree Women's Writing Group at the KSP Writers' Centre in 2009, and values their shared knowledge and friendships.

Since 2009, her work has been recognised in several competitions and anthology selections: local, nationally and internationally–both short stories and poetry.

In her non-writing life, Barbara has been a drummer, bagpiper, swimmer, secretary and debt collector, amongst other boring nouns.

An unusual 'claim to fame': in the 1960s, she defeated Bon Scott of AC/DC in a snare drumming competition prior to his notoriety. Barbara retains a program and medal as provenance.

Barbara likes nothing better than to tap away on the computer, creating stories worth remembering, enjoying the challenge of crafting characters and emotional storylines—most likely of the every-day person.

And, be warned, the unconscious creative voices haven't finished with her yet!

gurneybg@bigpond.net.au

www.barbaragurney.com

Other Works by the Author

Barbara's publications cover a diverse range of thought and application:

Fiction:

Road to Hanging Rock (2013)

The Promise (2017)

Ribbons of Love (2017)

Lessons of the Universe with Imogene Constantine (2019)

Dusty Heart (2020)

Doors of Prague (2021)

Short-Story Collections:

Purple and Other Hues (2018)

The Blue Book of Short Stories (2020)

The Green Book of Short Stories (2020)

Poetry:

Footprints of a Stranger (2012)

Life's Shadows (2015)

Seeking Self (2021)

About Dragonfly Publishing

Dragonfly Publishing is a boutique publisher and publishing services company based in the beautiful Perth Hills in Western Australia.

They aim to ensure an author's publishing journey is enjoyable and transformative, and pride themselves on their hand-holding ethos.

For more information, please see their website:

www.dragonflypublishing.com.au

To contact Dragonfly Publishing, please email:

info@dragonflypublishing.com.au

Printed in Australia
AUHW022232251022
370561AU00010B/785